SPARKLE

by Michele Amira
Foreword by Big Sean

Aliyah and Olivia keep on Sparkling!

Michele Amira

Sparkle
by Michele Amira

Edited by
Jodi Harris

Book Cover Illustration by
Sand One

Book Design by
Fred Yi

Photography by
Kwame Shaka Opare Photography

© 2014 Michele Amira, all rights reserved.
No part of this book may be reproduced or transmitted in any form
or by any means, electronic or mechanical, including photocopying,
recording or by any information storage and retrieval system,
without written permission from the author, except for the inclusion
of brief quotations in a review.

Printed in the United States of America
The Music in Me Foundation Int'l

GIFT
INSIDE
Free Downloads

*Go to www.themusicinme.org and visit
our store to receive your free downloads!*

978-0692264782

First Edition 2014

"To my Grandmama, Ginger Polansky, who taught me how to 'sparkle' through the best and worst times of life and for our days of shopping at Zara's and her blintze soufflé."
- Michele Amira

"I never paint dreams or nightmares. I paint my own reality."
- Frida Kahlo

Sparkle Shout Outs
✦ Playlist ✦

"Superwoman" by Alicia Keys:
To my mama, Jane Pinczuk, who is the wind beneath my wings and who has made it possible for me to "sparkle." I'm blessed to say, "I get it from my mama."

"Bonita Applebum" by A Tribe Called Quest:
Shout out to me and some of my favorite things—hip-hop, hairspray, hummus and hoop earrings!

"Black Synagogue" by Angel Haze:
To the fam, who makes me feel so safe like I'm in synagogue—my daddy Murray Pinczuk (who gave me his love for coffee), big "brotha" Sam Pinczuk, Grandmama Ginger Polansky; uncles Gregg Polansky and Emilio Pardo; Great Grandma Isabel Belarsky; aunts Sylvia Doyle, Iris Argueta, and Orli Jacobs.

"Hold You Down" by The Alchemist & Nina Sky:
For my favorite cousins and hipsters who hold me down— Alex Doyle, Mario Marsans, Mahyan Goldstein, Mana Eini, Jake Greenberg, Bethany Argueta and Moriah Jacobs.

"Jerusalem of Gold" by Naomi Shemer:
For my bubbie Fania Pinczuk who thought I was pretty enough to be Miss America. I miss you and your matzah ball soup! And my zadie Joseph Pinczuk who had so much swag! I miss you both!

"I Wonder if Heaven Got a Ghetto" by Tupac Shakur:
Shout out to my Uncle Michael, who is my namesake, and my granddad, who is the original OG granddad and my tap dancing partner. See you in heaven!

"Beautiful" by Christina Aguilera:
Shout out to Emily Clayton, my BFF foreves. Not even chemo, cancer, PICC lines or IVs could ruin your shine! You always sparkled even more than diamonds! See you in heaven, girla!

Sparkle Soundtrack

To listen to some of the bomb music that Diamond enjoys in *Sparkle*, please visit www.themusicinme.org. Click on our store menu and scroll down to access free music!

Special Sparkle Shout Out

"Starry Night" by Tupac Shakur:
Shout out to my favorite MC Big Sean for being such a "mensch" and writing the foreword for *Sparkle*. Tracks like "How It Feel" off his *Detroit* mixtape are an example of the power of hip-hop and G.O.O.D Music. Your influence is endless and profound!

It is amazing what can happen when one person stands up for another. We have seen this through history—small uprisings that change the face of nations. This is that uprising. Please visit our website at www.themusicinme.org for upcoming events and appearances. See how you can get involved.

Some Staggering Statistics:

- 1 in 7 students in grades K-12 are either a bully or a victim of bullying.

- 71% of students report incidents of bullying as a problem at their school.

- It is estimated that 160,000 children miss school every day due to fear of attack or intimidation by other students.

- 282,000 students are physically attacked in secondary schools each month.

- 90% of 4th through 8th graders report being victims of bullying.

Join the movement by helping UNITE AGAINST BULLYING. Please visit iTunes to purchase this amazing anthem, "Unleash Your Superpowers" by Don Trunk, feat. Uptown XO

Foreword

It is not easy growing up in today's world. Incidents of bullying, single parent families, academic pressures, drugs, and alcohol are prevalent almost everywhere. In *Sparkle*, author Michele Amira shows us and makes us feel the raw grittiness of what life is like for the youth of today.

Through the eyes of 14 year old Diamond Lopez, the story's main character, Michele exposes us to the emotional pain, anger, fears, and insecurities probably lurking somewhere in all of us. I, personally, know what it is like to be bullied, laughed at, teased, ridiculed, to have teachers shake their heads in pity, roll their eyes in disgust and tell me that my dream of being a rapper was ridiculous and unattainable. However, Diamond even has a further complication in her life. She is dealing with a life-threatening illness. As Diamond faces her physical challenges, we are educated about all of the emotions that accompany the thought of death and what it is like to live in excruciating physical pain. Ultimately, Diamond sets an example for us by "sparkling no matter what life has to offer."

This is an important book for everyone to read, especially middle schoolers. It is fanciful and funny enough to stimulate their imaginations, compelling enough to make them want to keep reading, and real enough to touch their hearts.

– Big Sean

Contents

Nothing Promised

Brrrring . . . Brrrring . . . Brrrring . . . Brrrring!

Diamond Lopez tried to hang onto sleep, despite the annoyingly loud phone ringing in the other room. After a few more Brrrrings, it stopped—either the caller gave up or her mother answered it.

The latter, she decided after a moment. She heard her mother say "hello" to someone.

Just another hour or so, Diamond thought with a wide yawn. *One more little hour of snooze time and . . .*

"No!" With a suddenly racing heart, the fourteen-year-old popped open her eyes and saw the light streaming in through the window. She took in the cherished posters of Jennifer Lopez, Jay-Z, Alicia Keys, Maroon 5, and The Beatles displayed on her bedroom walls, the latter placed strategically to cover up a patch of peeling paint. "Better get up. Move. Move. Move."

It was a windy morning at the beginning of Spring—the pink fluttering curtains attested to that. Ordinarily, she'd sleep in on a day like today . . . just because she could. No school today. No pressing obligations. No real reason to be up at any so-called reasonable hour. The pillow oh-so-soft and inviting and begging her to stay for just a little while longer.

Listen to the pillow, she thought. *One more hour of snooze time.*

But this was not an ordinary Saturday.

"No." The word came out as a groan this time.

She tried to shake off the sleep. It certainly wasn't an ordinary Saturday—it was exam day. And, as Diamond threw off the sluggishness, she grew nervous. Big nervous. In one last act of protest, she snuggled deep under her blankets and thought: *God, I hope I ace them. Please, please, please let me ace them. I can't be stuck in that gross high school up the street. I'll probably get my butt kicked every day if I have to go there. My friends aren't gonna be stuck there. No butt-kicking in their future. Please, please, please let me ace them.* She crossed and uncrossed her fingers for good measure and sucked in a deep breath, smelling a trace of the flower-scented fabric softener her mother used on the sheets.

"Please, please, please," she offered aloud. "Let me ace them."

Diamond—and everybody else in her Brooklyn

neighborhood—knew that Brooklyn Multicultural Collaborative School was reserved for the local thugs and lowlifes—the bottom of the barrel. No, worse than that . . . it was whatever the bottom of the barrel rested on. She desperately wanted to be saved—no, *needed* to be saved, *had to* be saved—from this fate worse than death by attending the smart kids' school, which was better known as Hunter College High School.

If she was accepted for next school year, it would mean traveling an additional fourteen subway stops away from her neighborhood. But this was definitely a trip she was prepared to make, even on a daily basis. What was a mere fourteen more stops when weighed against her entire future?

Nothing.

Fourteen more stops were absolutely nothing if it would keep her out of the bottom of the barrel and propel her to something better.

God, I hope I ace them, she thought again. *Please, please, please let me ace them.*

She knew she wasn't a natural test-taker, so she crossed her fingers again, so tight this time her knuckles turned white as she got out of bed and headed for the shower.

And that's when the first earth-shattering event of this day hit her with a cold, hard reality check. She saw the clock on her nightstand. It read 11:00. It felt like she'd been punched in the stomach; she'd planned on being up by 9.

"Oh no!" she screamed. "I can't believe I overslept! My nightmare of totally messing up my life has finally come true! Mama! Mamaaaaaaaa!"

Marsha Lopez, Diamond's thirty-year-old mother, didn't answer.

"Mama! Where *are* you?"

It took Diamond a moment to realize that her mother was speaking in a muffled voice on the phone in their cramped galley kitchen. It took her only another moment to toss the rest of her manners out the window. She ran over to her mother and rudely interrupted the conversation.

"How could you let me oversleep?" she demanded. "This is a disaster! Now I'm going to be stuck at—"

Marsha, deeply involved in the phone call, turned her back to Diamond. She covered the telephone receiver with the palm of her hand and whispered: "Look at the clock on the wall, Niña." She gestured to it with a tip of her head. "You still have plenty of time. I need to have some privacy right now, so go get ready. ¡Apúrate!"

Diamond saw the clock and a wave of relief washed over her. She realized what had happened. Her own Art Deco style clock radio had stopped at 11 . . . last night. Usually, she woke to the sound of her favorite hip-hop station blaring into her ears. But the batteries obviously had gone dead. As dead as her manners.

"Sorry," she said so softly that her mother couldn't hear. "Sorry. Sorry. Sorry. I just don't want to end up at the bottom of the barrel."

Still, Diamond felt only a little ashamed for bellowing at her mother like that, cutting herself some slack for the momentousness of today. She figured she would apologize properly later, after the exams. Apologize with some meaning in the words. After her future was sealed.

Please, please, please let me ace them.

Right now, she didn't have time to dwell on politeness. Instead, she decided to dwell on filling her stomach, which was grumbling from more than just nerves. She proceeded to pig out on her favorite breakfast of dry Frosted Flakes and buttery sunny-side-up eggs while Marsha finished the phone call in the privacy of her bedroom.

Finished eating, Diamond grabbed her backpack and ran out the door.

"Wish me luck, Mama!" A hug for good luck would have been nice, Diamond thought. But her mother was still yakking away to whoever was on the phone. Her mother did hold up a finger, one of those "give me a moment" gestures. But Diamond couldn't wait. "Gotta go. Bye!"

Marsha called out from behind the bedroom door, "I love you Niña! Good luck!"

She said something else, but Diamond didn't hear, as she was already on her way to the rumbling overhead subway stop near their apartment, her feet pounding in time to the clackity-clacks, her breath puffing away like the hissing belches of the train.

Diamond lived a few blocks from the Atlantic Ocean in Brighton Beach. It was a short stroll down the boardwalk to Brighton Beach's freaky cousin Coney Island, where Diamond and her friends usually hung out . . . which is where she might be on any other Saturday. During baseball season, they liked to go to MCU Park to watch the Cyclones play ball in a dilapidated section of the island. She wasn't allowed to go there by herself. A few blocks in the other direction was the F stop, and that's where she was headed at breakneck pace this morning.

As Diamond skidded to a halt, she noticed that all the usual characters were present: Guido playas, baggy pants guys giving each other thug hugs, pungent street people begging for change, maids on their way to clean the houses of the rich in the suburbs, some of the other locals from Diamond's hood and, as always, lecherous old men checking out her nicely shaped J.Lo booty and her well-endowed chest. She shoved all of them to the back of her mind, daydreamed that she was dancing to "How It Feel" by one of her favorite MCs, Big Sean, and waited. She wondered if her friends had taken the subway or had sprung for a cab to the school. Not a one of them was in sight at the moment.

Please, please, please let me ace them.

Although Diamond had lots of friends, she also spent a lot of time alone, either listening to music or making music. It had been that way for as long as she could remember. Her stereo or TV constantly blared hip-hop, pop, rock and reggaeton, and "Please! Diamond! Turn it down!" was a familiar sentiment echoing through the Lopez family's tiny rent-controlled apartment. When Diamond was five, she loved to dance around their small living room in her pink ballet leotard. She pretended to be one of those little girls on the Upper East Side who enrolled in ballet lessons and performed in pretty sequined costumes in front of their parents. Diamond would swirl around for what seemed like hours sometimes, barely touching the floor. Anybody would believe she'd been taking dance lessons most of her life. She often whined to her mom, "I've never been to ONE dance lesson! It's not fair!" Then she'd pout, and Marsha would reassure her, "Baby, I hope you realize you're a very gifted dancer."

Diamond knew this, even from a young age, but she wanted to be a *better* dancer. A better dancer would have a better chance to be popular, to hang out with the coolest kids and to be noticed, not invisible.

Sometimes, Diamond felt practically invisible. Not one of the locals waiting for the train had so much as given her a nod this morning. She glanced down, studying the tips of her shoes and focusing on the muted sound of an oldies rock station spilling out of someone's iPod.

As Diamond grew older, she still danced—when her mother wasn't watching—and music became her escape from difficult times. She fell in love with hip-hop, reggaeton, rock, and rap and many other kinds of music, and watched music videos constantly, fascinated by the musicians and their beautiful video vixens. She was glued to music magazines and was always up-to-speed on the latest trends in the music industry.

C'mon, c'mon, she urged. *Where's the train?*

But music wasn't everything; she was also crazy about comic books, and fantasized about the true existence of superheroes like Storm, Wolverine, and Superman—heroes who could save her from pain and suffering—superheroes who never had to wait for the F train or take tests. It was Diamond's secret desire to be her own version of a superhero–a Nuyorican, a New York born Puerto Rican big booty super girl. Diamond believed that her booty was one of her best attributes and, based on this fact, she created her own comic hero and alter ego, *Nuyorican Knockout,* a big booty supergirl who could save the world from evil.

Nuyorican Knockout got her name from her super hot good looks, but also from the fact that she could literally knock her opponents out by gyrating her hips and booty with such power that it launched them off the planet. The shaking and grinding of her shapely bottom . . . Nuyorican always dressed in miniskirts, stiletto heels, and blinding bling . . . distracted her enemies and put them into a trance. Her butt was also used for supersonic transportation. Much like a huge bouncy ball, she could bounce her booty on the ground and launch herself into the sky to fly for miles.

Diamond wished she could fly to the school this morning for the exams.

WHERE WAS THE TRAIN? Had she just missed it? If she had to wait for the next, she might be late.

When she wasn't thinking about music and dance, Diamond spent a lot of time channeling Nuyorican Knockout, especially when she walked to the Neptune Avenue subway on her way to school and the local men would holler out: "Mmmmmm, I'd like to get me a piece o' dat." She'd fix her big brown eyes on whatever book she had in her hands, appearing to ignore the cat calls, but in a twisted way she listened to them. She liked how they made her feel. She also liked the idea of Nuyorican Knockout ejecting those men to outer space.

Little did those scumbags know who they were messing with, because Nuyorican Knockout possessed a power far too great for them to handle. Standing on the platform and trying for a change to shut out the leering men, Diamond continued to imagine herself as Nuyorican Knockout. She'd put her hand on her mighty booty and say, "You like this? Well, take that!"

And then, while gyrating her hips, the ground would begin

to shake and the scumbags would be so hypnotized that they'd have no idea of the danger that they were about to face. BOOM! BOOM! POW! Her hips would hit them with such torque that the men would go flying into Queens and wouldn't even know what hit them!

****

Once safely on the train, the combination of the car's motion and Kanye West's song "Good Life" playing on Diamond's iPod calmed her and moved her into the zone.

God, please let me ace them, she thought again. *Please, please, please.* She would have added *let me ace them and I'll never ask for anything else.* But she knew she'd ask for something and so kept the promise out of the mental equation.

By the time she got to school, she was donning game face and felt a bit more relaxed. But as soon as she walked into the testing room and feasted her eyes on Adam Harrison—the hottie she'd been crushing on all year—her heart starting pounding again.

Adam was a real bad boy and an up-and-coming rapper, or so Diamond believed. He was in her math class. He was her age, which was a year older than just about everyone else seated at the desks, maybe even a year older than that, as she was pretty sure he shaved. All the girls loved him, or at least wanted to hook up with him. He had a dangerous combination of charisma and sex appeal, which would easily explain Diamond's inability to pay attention to her math class. It wasn't just his looks that made Diamond's heart skip a few beats. He exuded a cool factor that was off the scale. He had a smile that belonged on one of those "Got Milk?" billboards. He had a voice to complete the package—nothing nasally, like some of the other boys in math. It was radio DJ-quality, sultry and distinct, with just a dash of coyness thrown in.

But mostly Diamond had fixated on him because he wasn't younger than her—she figured he was the only boy in this middle school who wasn't.

I'm screwed, she thought. *How am I gonna concentrate on this stupid test? He looks totally fresh to death!*

As she shuffled past him, she worked up the courage to smile and say, "Hi." Then she found a seat and tried not to lose herself in a sexual fantasy involving Mr. Bad Boy—the code name she used when discussing Adam with her friends.

I wish I wasn't such wasn't such a loser around boys, she mused. *It's gotta be easier than this. If only I was prettier! If only I was Nuyorican Knockout! THE TEST!* she scolded.

Even with all the distraction Mr. Bad Boy provided, this test really meant something to her, and she couldn't afford to lose focus.

Don't look.

Don't look at him.

Don't look at Mr. Bad Boy.

That's it. I'm not gonna even look at his shoes. He's not in the same room with me now. He's on the moon. He's farther away than the moon. It's only me and this test, she repeated to herself again and again. *Nuyorican Knockout has booted him off the planet and into another solar system to keep me out of the bottom-of-the-barrel school.*

Hours passed, or so it seemed, and finally the test was over. She breathed a sigh of relief as she walked down the hall. Mr. Bad Boy had strutted out of the classroom first, the questions probably dirt-simple to him. How much earlier had he finished? So many questions on the test were still racing through her mind, especially from the math section. It made her stomach churn.

Those probability questions were so confusing. They actually hurt my brain! Like, who actually cares if "Joey" has 15 red and 17 blue marbles in a bag? And who cares about "Joey's" chances of pulling out a blue marble if he reaches in without looking? Why does anyone need to know about the chance that he might get a red one instead? If he kept the blue marble out, is he more likely to pull out another blue marble, or a red one? And what about the marbles jumbling up my head? How many are there and when will they explode right through the holes of my pathetically lame brain. Oh God, I hope I didn't blow the test. No, I think I did okay. But, maybe I didn't. Maybe there was a green marble in my bag. A big green honkin' marble.

Just then, her thoughts were interrupted by the sound of someone behind her saying, "See you in math Monday."

She spun around to see that it was Adam. The big booty girl couldn't believe it. He must have been hanging out in the hall, and she was so caught up with the marbles she hadn't noticed walking by him.

Oh my God, he spoke to me first! she thought, almost speaking out loud as he glided past her with a sly smile. *Mr. Bad Boy spoke to me. Mr. Bad Boy smiled at me.*

She rode the train home in a daze. All she could do was look forward to her next encounter with Mr. Bad Boy—the tall, thin, gorgeous black Jewish dude with sensitive hazel eyes who talked to her first today. Thinking about him kept her from worrying about the exam. Well, kept her from worrying as much as she had been worrying. God, but he looked so good in those baggy pants. Her stomach wasn't in quite as many knots as it had been earlier.

When she returned home, Diamond plopped onto the couch and hollered, "Mama! I'm back!" Softer: "If you care that I'm back. If you're not still yakkin' on the phone, I'm back. If you're curious about my day and the test and the . . ." Louder: "Mama!"

No answer.

"Mama? Where are you?"

A moment later Marsha appeared from her bedroom and tentatively asked, "So . . . how was it? The test?"

Diamond shrugged. "Not too bad, I guess. Not as bad as I thought it might be." She tried to keep from glowing about Mr. Bad Boy.

"As usual, I'm ecstatically proud of you," her mom said. Diamond thought her mother was especially fond of that word—ecstatically—and managed to use it at least once a day. Her mother was always trying to slip a big word into a conversation, even when it didn't call for it or the word didn't quite fit. Her mother lacked a real high school education, having dropped out during her sophomore year and later getting a GED. She'd even taken a couple of community college courses, probably where she picked up the big words. "I knew you'd do exceedingly well."

Despite her mother's cheerful-sounding words, the facial expression didn't match. Her mom couldn't hide her puffy, tear-stained cheeks.

"Something wrong, Mama?"

No answer.

"What's wrong, Mama?" Diamond insisted, a hint of worry and ire creeping into her voice. "You all right?" Maybe the phone call this morning was about some relative dying.

"Don't worry about it. Nothing's wrong. I'm fine." Marsha ran her fingers through her hair and let out a breath. "Let's have Chinese carryout tonight, to celebrate your test, and we can have some girl talk."

Diamond gave her a limp smile. "Not tonight, Mama. I was

thinking of hanging out with Shayna at her house. Okay if I go over there? I won't stay out too late."

Marsha shook her head, her curls drifting down to her eyebrows. "Diamond, you can be with your friend another time. Let's have a girls' night. It'll be fun."

"No way!" Diamond smacked her lips, replying a little too harshly. "I deserve this night with Shayna! After the work, the test, I want to—"

Diamond stopped when Marsha sighed in frustration. She saw the disappointment screaming volumes in her mother's eyes. Normally, Diamond would nag her mother relentlessly until she'd cave in—and she thought this time wouldn't be any different. Her mother always caved. But there was something in her mother's eyes that stopped the argument she was continuing to form. This time, Diamond realized a "girls' night" was really important.

"Okay, Mama. I guess I'll see Shayna tomorrow. A girls' night it is."

She could tell that her mother was surprised that she gave in so easily. And despite Marsha's smile, Diamond could sense the tense body language; Diamond didn't usually miss a thing. Her mother was sad about something. A death somewhere in the family, she decided. Or some old friend or lost love or somesuch. *Maybe she'll get around to telling me who over Chinese.* Though she and her mom often argued, Diamond was ultimately sensitive and aimed to please. She wouldn't press her mother for the details now.

"I'll have the General Tzo's," Diamond said.

While they waited for the food to be delivered, Diamond retreated to her bedroom, where a gentle ocean breeze blew through her window and brought with it a slightly salty scent that cut the pong of the neighborhood. She sang and danced around her bed to Jay-Z's "Show Me What You Got." She never got tired of singing and watching herself perform in the mirror as she shook her booty, thrust her hips, flipped her hair, and seductively wiggled to the music. A fellow Brooklynite, Jay-Z had a vibe that connected deeply with Diamond. As she continued to strut her stuff around her room, she entertained a few lustful thoughts about Adam.

Buzz . . . Buzz . . . Buzz . . . Buzz . . .

"Food's here!" Marsha called. "I just buzzed in the delivery man. He'll be up soon, Niña. C'mon and get it while it's hot."

Or at least lukewarm, Diamond thought as she danced into the kitchen to find her mother setting the table and nervously dropping utensils all over the floor.

"Mama . . . what's up with you?" Diamond bent over to pick up a spoon and some forks. "You're actin' kinda weird, and it's creepin' me out. You all right?"

Marsha's smile looked forced. "Don't worry. I'm fine. Really,

I'm fine. Let's eat before it gets cold and I have to nuke it in the microwave. It's never quite as good nuked."

Diamond was excruciatingly hungry. Chinese carryout was a real treat, since they ate in most of the time to save money—home-cooked meals from ingredients her mother picked up at the local Russian market. She craved New York-style Chinese food, especially General Tzo's Chicken, which really rocked, even though she could never be sure if the deep-fried spicy chicken was actually chicken or tofu. She took a sip of her Dr. Pepper and watched her mom pull out a bubbling Mrs. Smith Dutch Apple Crumb Pie from the oven for dessert.

"Hey, Mama . . . do you suppose Dr. Pepper is really a doctor and, if so, what kind? And do you think Mrs. Smith and Dr. Pepper would ever get together, or is she more of a Mr. Pibb kinda girl?" Diamond chuckled at her own joke.

"Mr. Pibb sounds kinda pimpish to me. I think she'd go for the doctor," Marsha answered with a broken smile. "If Mrs. Smith isn't already taken. You have such a way with words!"

"Awesome sauce." Diamond wolfed down an egg roll and the rest of her food as she spoke with a stuffed mouth, the words a little muffled. "This is really good."

"I'm ecstatic that you like it."

"You know, Mama, my life would rock if I got into Hunter College High School! I'd feel so good about myself. You think I'll get in?"

"I hope so. We'll have to wait and see." Marsha stared out the window.

Diamond only half-noticed that her mother stirred her food and wasn't eating.

"I understand, Mama. But waiting is so hard! I need to count on something so I can plan next year. Besides, I know Shayna and Tamara will probably get in. In fact, I'm sure they'll get in. What would I do without them? Especially in a school that sucks? I don't want to go to a school that sucks. I don't want . . ."

Marsha said, "Niña, you worry too much. You're going to have to be patient. It'll be okay."

"How long before I know my score? I didn't ask, didn't think about it. I should have asked when I turned the test in. How long do you think it'll take them to go through all the answers and—"

"Niña, give it a rest. Everything will turn out fine. It'll be okay."

"Fine. Okay." Words her mother was using too much.

For some reason, Diamond didn't find her mother's words reassuring. In fact, they sounded unconvincing, shallow, like her mother was talking in this room but was somewhere far beyond the apartment and the city. On the moon. In another solar system. Bopped there by Nuyorican Knockout for saying "fine" and "okay" one too many times.

Why was her mother so preoccupied?

Setting her concern aside, Diamond instead imagined her dad comforting and encouraging her. He wouldn't be on another planet on a night like this.

Papa would know what to tell me. He'd make sure that I got into Hunter College High School. In fact, we'd have so much money that I wouldn't have to worry about being in a trashy school anymore. Wait, I'd probably go to Dalton, shop on Fifth Avenue, live in a penthouse and go to lots of Jay-Z concerts. I wouldn't have to take the subway ever again, and I'd be driven to school in a limo by our own private driver. I'd be one of the "beautiful people" and everything would be perfect. I'd be Papa's little girl, and he'd take care of my mom and me forever. And when mom said 'okay,' it would be because everything really was okay. More than okay.

****

Diamond stopped herself from having a second piece of pie. No use making the booty too, too bootilicous. She finally realized her mother hadn't touched a bite of it . . . or a single bite of anything.

Some mother-daughter dinner.

And some attempt on her mother's part to have a "girls' night." The food had been good, but the company too distracted. Diamond wished she'd pressed for going to Shayna's after all. It would have been more fun. She was just about to open her mouth and issue a taunt to that effect when she noticed that her mother's eyes were watery and her face was all red. Gone was all trace of the feigned lightheartedness.

"Mama?"

Marsha started to say something, but her voice cracked.

"Mama—"

"I . . . I don't know—"

"Don't know what, Mama? What's going on? Who died? An old friend? Some uncle or aunt? Some cousin I've never met? What's happened?" This time Diamond's thoughts didn't wander. She fixed her mother with a steely gaze that as much as said, "I ain't backing down this time." Diamond pushed her empty plate away. "Mama, what's wrong?"

"I don't know how to tell you this. I want you to know everything will be fine. It'll be okay."

Fine. Okay. It wasn't a "fine, okay" voice her mother used. It was a sad, nervous, something-is-wrong-and-I'm-holding-back voice. It was a terrible voice that Diamond rarely heard and never liked.

"Tell me what?" Diamond pressed, her eyes daggers that said she wasn't backing down this time. "What?"

Marsha started to cry.

"Mama! Oh my God! What's wrong? Just tell me!" Diamond stood up so fast from the table she knocked her chair over. "Are you sick? Is it *Abuela?* Grandma? Please tell me. You're making it worse by not telling me. Mama!"

Eighty percent, Diamond suddenly thought. *Eighty-friggin-percent.*

Diamond couldn't swallow and fought for breath. All the once-pleasant smells of the kitchen—the Chinese spices, the apple pie—were suddenly suffocating. A large lump tightly wedged into her throat.

Eighty percent. Dear God, please please please let me still be eighty percent.

"Mama, please, you have to tell me." But in that instant, Diamond realized she really didn't want to know. She wanted to be in the eightieth percentile, and she didn't want any words that might shatter that.

She wanted to run and hide.

Instead, she took a deep breath, bracing herself for what she knew would most certainly be bad news. "Mama?" The word came out as a croaking whisper.

Am I in the twentieth percentile?

Marsha edged away from the table and took Diamond's hand, speaking in such a barely audible tone.

"I didn't hear you, Mama. What's—"

Marsha squared her shaking shoulders. "I was talking to Dr. Goldberg this morning on the phone when you woke up."

Twenty percent. Nineteen, eighteen, seventeen, sixteen. I'm fourteen and might never see fifteen . . .

The lump in Diamond's throat swelled larger. "Mama—"

"He told me you had a relapse…"

Diamond froze.

The room started spinning out of control and she struggled to stay on her feet. She hadn't felt sick. Not until that moment.

"Relapse? What? It can't be! The leukemia is back? But I passed the seven-year mark! I feel fine. I feel good. There must be a mistake. I don't believe it. Maybe someone misread the results, or maybe they're not mine. That's it. They're not mine! There's nothing wrong with me! I passed the seven-year mark! Seven years!"

Diamond knew the statistics, had read about them through the past seven years. She knew people with her cancer had an eighty percent survival rate after the five-year mark. She knew that the longer she made it past her initial diagnosis and treatment, the greater her survival chances.

"Mama, eighty percent. The odds were in my favor."

Marsha's face took on a calm mask, but Diamond saw through it. There was no calm, only despair. She fell into her mother's arms, and they both burst into tears. Time seemed to stand still at that moment, yet it was rushing by at the speed of light. Their shoulders shook.

"I'm scared, Mama."

"It will be all right."

Fine. Okay.

"What am I gonna do?" Diamond wept.

"We'll get through this together, Niña." The words came out in a soothing voice, but they did nothing to sooth Diamond. "That's what we'll do, get through this. It'll be okay. Don't worry, baby, we'll—"

Diamond replied sharply, "We . . . no! I think you meant ME! ME! Will YOU be in pain? Will YOU lose your hair? Will YOU be hooked up to IVs and poked to death until your veins collapse? Will YOU puke your guts out? Will YOU be away from your friends? Will YOU lose another year in school 'cause you miss too many classes?" Will YOU be one more year older than everyone else in your grade? Two years older now? No! *I* will! ME. ME. ME."

An uncomfortable silence settled in the kitchen, and the once-wonderful smells of Chinese spices and apple pie twisted into something horrible and monstrous and so overpowering it made Diamond gag. Outside a car horn blared, a dog barked, someone whistled. Music came faintly from somewhere, a hip-hop tune that Diamond knew by heart but suddenly couldn't remember a single word.

"Niña, what I mean is that I'm here for you. Of course you're right . . . it's a journey only you can travel. But I'll be in the passenger's seat for the whole ride. So let's fasten our seatbelts. We can do this, baby. *You* can do this. I know you can. You *will*.

Everything's going to be fine, I know it. It'll be okay. Everything's— "

Fine. Okay.

Someone changed the station, and Diamond thought she recognized Beyoncé crooning away. Calming a little and wiping the tears from her cheeks, she shook her head. "That's corny, Mama. The passenger seat? You know we're in for a hell of a ride. And it's gonna suck."

They both smiled just a little, and Diamond suspected her mother's was as fake as hers. The stress was so thick in the room it was a palpable field that not even Nuyorican Knockout could cross. It was crushing. Diamond felt incredibly weak, newborn puppy weak, smacked by a train weak. She extricated herself from her mother's embrace and went to the living room to stretch out on the couch. She couldn't hear the music in here.

"When do I have to go into the hospital? And for how long?" Diamond asked after a few moments had passed. "What do I tell my friends?"

Her mother stood in the doorway. "Tell your friends the truth, Niña. Tell them—"

"Tell them I might die? Tell them that I'm in the twenty percent of people who can't shake the Big C?"

"Niña—"

"I don't want them to know!" Diamond interrupted. "I don't

want everybody at school looking at me like I'm 'leukemia girl.' They'll stay away. Who wants to touch 'leukemia girl?' I certainly wouldn't want to. It might rub off. They might catch it. I don't wanna be a disease again. I hate this!"

Marsha rocked forward on the balls of her feet and interlocked her fingers. "Diamond, it won't be like that. You have to tell Shayna and Tamara, at least. You'll need their support. They need to know. Remember how much you loved getting visitors in the hospital? Last time, you were only seven, but now you're older, wiser and stronger, and things will be different. I know that everything's going to be just fine."

"Just fine?" She shuddered at the thought of all the needles. "Fine. Okay."

"Besides, Spring Break isn't all that far away. So you won't have to worry about school for awhile. I bet you're not going to miss much."

And that thought's supposed to make me feel better?

****

Diamond lay awake all night, listening to the waves rolling in on the shore and the occasional interruption of a car door slamming. She was plagued by thoughts of the future. Would there be a future?

I can't believe all that time passed in remission, and I was finally able to relax and think I had a future. Thought I might be ninety percent. One hundred percent free and clear. But now I'm totally blindsided. I don't think I have what it takes to go through this crap again! I don't want to go through this again. Last time, I was seven. I was too young to know better. This is going to screw up my entire life, if I have one left at all. Another year behind in school, maybe, and that's if I survive. I'm already a year older than my best friends. ONE MORE YEAR BEHIND. There's so much I want to do. Survive. Will I even survive? I don't want to JUST survive. I want to really live, and not as an anonymous virgin! Roll up your sleeve, Diamond. We need to take a little blood, Diamond. Take a deep breath, Diamond, this won't hurt much. Everything will be fine, Diamond. Everything will be okay, Diamond.

"Everything will suck."

She glanced at the clock, realizing her mother must have put in new batteries. It was 3 a.m. She stretched an arm over and picked up her phone to call Shayna. Diamond knew she was blessed to have her own phone at her age . . . the only thing she considered herself blessed with for the moment. A splurge her mother had allowed.

"Pick up. Pick up."

When she heard her friend's sleepy voice on the other end of the line, she burst out weeping so badly that she could hardly speak.

"Hello . . . hello? Is anyone there?" Shayna grumbled. "Who is this? You creep. I'm going to hang up—"

Diamond managed to squeeze out, "Shayna, don't hang up—"

Her friend replied, "Is this a prank or somethin'? Who is this?"

"Wait! It's me, Diamond. I have to talk to you! I know it's late . . . early . . . I'm so sorry. I have to talk."

Diamond heard a long yawn from the other end, a signal that Shayna was beginning to wake up. "Diamond? What's wrong? You worried about that test today? It was just a test."

Diamond took a deep breath so that she could squeeze her voice out. "It's back, Shayna. It's come back. It's come back and I can't handle this. I don't want to handle this. I don't want it to be real. What am I gonna to do? What's gonna happen to me? How can I tell people? What about Adam? It's back. What about school? What about my life? It's back."

Diamond knew Shayna had no idea what she was blathering about. Her words continued rapid-fire until she took a breath.

"What's back?" came Shayna's sleepy voice.

"My leukemia is back, Shayna." And then she totally lost it, crying uncontrollably, so hard that her whole body bounced against the mattress and she worried that she would wake up her mother in the other room.

There was silence on the other end. What *could* Shayna say? Diamond thought. She hadn't known Shayna when she was seven and had leukemia the first time, but she'd told Shayna about it. She told Shayna about practically everything. Shayna was a year younger . . . all of her school friends were a year younger because of the time she'd lost to the first go-round with the disease.

Diamond wanted her friend to offer profound, comforting words, but nothing save dead air came through the phone. Then Diamond heard something. Shayna had started crying, too.

The two girls shared a crying fest, exhausting themselves and finally settling into a conversation about school and Mr. Bad Boy and the exam, until Diamond stammered, "I-I-I have to go."

Shayna answered, "I'll tell Tamara. I'm so sorry."

Shayna was a true best friend. She didn't say everything would be fine or okay.

"I am so very sorry, Dia—"

"So am I." Diamond hung up.

All the wonderful things that Diamond was looking forward to in her life, like going to a new school, were coming to a close in one awful, horrible, lousy night of hideous stupidity and totally broken dreams.

Nuyorican Knockout urgently hopped onto her purple swag surfer, all decked out in sleek Versace couture. As she transformed herself into a microscopic big booty mini-skirted superhero, she surfed throughout Diamond's bloodstream, destroying all the leukemic cells in her path by blasting hip-hop music at them. With every

*thunderous, pulsating beat from Knockout's swag surfer,
the diseased cells exploded into oblivion and didn't have
a chance.*

*"Take that! And this! You ain't no match for me.
I'll knock you out!"*

*But the tables quickly turned as the leukemic
cells rapidly multiplied around her, accumulating
in Diamond's bone marrow and gobbling up all the
good cells. They also became resistant to Knockout's
earthquaking hip-hop beats.*

*"What's going on here? You can't get through my
force field!"*

*But the cells nonetheless boldly broke through
Knockout's protective shield and started draining her
powers by entering her system through every pore in
her body.*

*In defeat, Nuyorican Knockout realized she
needed to regroup to come up with a new plan of attack
to save Diamond. She pushed the hyperdrive button to
the start position on her swag surfer and jetted away
from the imposing danger . . . for now.*

Blue Hair

Diamond didn't want to be Diamond . . . not now.

And she hadn't wanted to be Diamond then.

Seven years ago, she wanted to be just about anyone else. Anywhere else.

Seven years ago, she was obsessed with fame and fortune, dreaming of being a movie star or a rock singer or a super model wearing flashy clothes and strutting to the latest music with cameras flashing and people ooohing and ahhhing and pointing and clapping. Posters of her grinning visage taped up on young girls' bedroom walls. Her mug spotted in magazine pages and on billboards. Diamond would be a cover girl like Drew Barrymore. She would be a sexy DJ on HOT 97, hip-hop's freshest station in NY. She would be a star one way or another. Her life was going to mean something, and she was going to leave a big, splashy mark on the world.

Seven years ago, she also remembered coming down with what she thought was a bad case of the flu. And soon fervently wishing it had been the flu.

Praying for the flu.

Sadly, seven years ago her diagnosis had turned out to be a lot more severe and devastating.

Lymphoblastic leukemia, better known as childhood leukemia, were the two words the doctor had said repeatedly.

Lymphoblastic leukemia, the syllables sounding to Diamond like a heavy door slamming or a guillotine blade dropping. The words attached themselves to her tongue and she learned how to spell them when she'd had trouble at school with spelling far simpler things.

L-y-m-p-h-o-b-l-a-s-t-i-c l-e-u-k-e-m-i-a.

It was a form of cancer usually affecting kids between two and ten years of age and Diamond, at seven, had fit in the range rather nicely. Like other kids with this disease, Diamond was highly susceptible to infections, with little or no defense against them. She was sickly—skinny, scared, pale, and pained.

Although the cancer had gone into remission after a year, right after her eighth birthday, she worried. She was considered "cured," as far as all the doctors said. But she complained often to her mother about her fears. Well, she never voiced *all* of them, but there were so many that some of them bubbled to the top of her young brain and rattled out and around the tiny apartment.

She trembled every time she got a runny nose.

Her heart seized when she sneezed.

Headaches? Colds? They put her stomach in knots.

"Cured, Mom? I don't think I'll ever feel cured," she remembered saying practically every day for the longest time. Hadn't she read in some magazine in the doctor's office that, once you have cancer, you *always* have cancer . . . it was just a matter of keeping it knocked down. She had to live with her "cured" cancer every waking moment, and usually recalled dreaming about it at night. *Cancer. Cancer. Cancer*. The word followed her everywhere like a mantra, and for the longest time movies and music and friends did little to camouflage it. The slightest cough sent her head to spinning because she worried the cancer was back.

Cured, supposedly, Diamond thought back then, but she hadn't felt like it. She still felt sick. Her mom said "that's all in your head." Maybe, she'd thought. Maybe not.

"When will I feel normal again? Ever?" she'd remembered asking. "Being sick sucks big time!" Her feelings at the time were pretty grown-up for someone of her few years, and she imagined that she was lugging around a huge time bomb that was ready to explode at any moment. And the time bomb would release cancer particles all over her. "It sucks, Mom."

Marsha always replied with a faint smile and a pat on the head. "I know exactly what you mean."

But she didn't know. Marsha couldn't possibly know because the cancer hadn't been inside her. Every time her mom tried to comfort her, Diamond would roll her eyes toward the sky and nod. *Sure you know what I mean*, she thought then.

Sure you know what I mean now.

Cancer was a burden—the thought and threat of it, the very clunky, dangerous sound of the word, and Diamond carried this burden around with her. Even at eight, the "cured" Diamond understood the seriousness of that one horrible, lousy, rotten word, and the car-door slamming guillotine-dropping terror of the two words *lymphoblastic leukemia*.

She understood about sickness and dying and no happily-ever-after.

But as the years went by, the burden lessened. There'd been no secondary malignancies. It became less and less likely for a relapse . . . her doctor had rattled off the statistics, and she'd found some measure of hope in them. Diamond let herself enjoy things and embrace her childhood. She turned the music up, danced more, laughed often, and smiled at the slightest thing. When she passed the five-year-mark and made the magical eighty percent survival rate, then hit the six-year mark, and then the seven, it was like the burdened had disappeared, she been a caterpillar that had morphed into a beautiful butterfly.

Time to spread her gossamer wings.

Lymphoblastic leukemia fell out of her vocabulary.

But it all came back in full force today, a brick wall she'd run into at the proverbial full-tilt.

Now the nightmare was back in spades, the two words swirling in her head and threatening to choke out all her other thoughts. Lymphoblastic leukemia. Lymphoblastic leukemia. Lymphoblastic leukemia. The news of the relapse—on a day that started out with great potential, a day that could see her crawling out of the bottom-of-the-barrel school for losers—shattered her world.

Lymphoblastic leukemia sucked bigger than big time.

She hoped she'd aced her tests, and beyond that she'd hoped she might have a chance with Adam, Mr. Bad Boy. He'd spoken first to her, after all. He'd smiled at her, too, hadn't he? She hadn't imagined that "Got Milk?" smile.

Life was just getting good . . . and now this. It sucked!

It sucked worse than it had seven years ago. Yeah, seven years ago she understood the seriousness of the disease. But seven years ago, she'd been too young to think about avoiding rubbing grimy elbows with the local thugs and lowlifes at MS 40. She'd been too young to think about a better school and Mr. Bad Boy . . . who probably would look the other way when cancer-girl walked by.

Life was getting good and "remission" was the number one word in her mental vocabulary. R-e-m-i-s-s-i-o-n.

She'd nearly suppressed the memory of battling a disease that had nearly killed her.

Might indeed kill her now.

She'd gamely confronted her fears each time she had to return to New York-Presbyterian Morgan Stanley Children's Hospital for "routine" follow up appointments, some of which hurt and most of which secretly terrified her.

Now, once again, Diamond and her mother would have to trudge back to that same hospital for the treatment she dreaded. Pain and weakness and uncertainty. Would it be worse because she was older and smarter, better understood all the ramifications of the disease and now knew well in advance about the so-called-battery-of-tests and needles and bags of chemicals-dubbed-drugs that would be fed into her veins? Expensive poison. Would it be easier because she knew what to expect? Did she really know what to expect?

Dear God, why couldn't it be someone else this was happening to?

Why couldn't she be someone else?

Would it be . . . different this time? Easier? Worse? Because she was older, would the treatments be more aggressive . . . rougher? Would she get weaker? Would the pain be tougher to manage? Or would it maybe not hurt quite so much this go-round? Was pain worse to a seven-year-old than to a fourteen-year-old? Would her stomach feel like the inside of a washing machine on the spin cycle? Would her head feel like an old pair of tennis shoes thumping around in the dryer? Would she keep food down? Would it . . .

Would it . . .

Would it . . .

Would it . . .

Be unexpected?

Expecting the unexpected was more than Diamond could bear.

She couldn't sleep a wink the night before the morning ride to the hospital. Her head swam with thoughts of her upcoming initial chemotherapy treatment. God, chemotherapy. A word that ranked way up there in the charts with lymphoblastic leukemia. C-h-e-m-o-t-h-e-r-a-p-y.

She hadn't allowed herself to call her friends, because she was afraid she wouldn't talk to them, not even to Shayna, would only cry and appear weak before the drugs truly made her weak. She hadn't allowed herself to think about Mr. Bad Boy or Hunter College High School, where she'd really rather be right now . . . rather than in this hospital . . . even though she was indeed thinking about Mr. Bad Boy now and Hunter College High School.

She'd rather be anywhere else, even at the bottom of the

educational barrel school. Even at the bottom of what the bottom of the barrel sat on.

Be anyone else.

Dr. Goldberg explained to Diamond—via Marsha—that the hospital stay would range between two weeks and a month. Diamond figured that meant at least a month, depending on her reactions to the drugs. He said she wouldn't miss another year of school . . . not this time.

But what if the doctor was lying? What if she did miss more school? What if she . . .

Papa, I know you're out there. Please help me. We need you . . . I need you.

Diamond felt trapped in endless bleakness and despair, imagined herself as a watercolor painting where the artist had used too much water and everything had run together like a rainbow of tears, a sidewalk chalk drawing muted by rain. Everything was blurry. She whimpered and tossed and turned like a baby, sticking her fist in her mouth so her mother wouldn't hear her cry.

She should've eaten breakfast, but she "took a pass" on it, and her mother didn't argue.

They rode in silence in the back seat of the cab. It smelled like someone had gotten sick in it and that air freshener had been poured on the cracked vinyl seats to cover it up. The melding of odors—

coupled with Diamond's nervous stomach—threatened to bring up last night's dinner.

Her mother only made a weak attempt at conversation and gracefully did not force the issue.

When they passed Broadway show billboards blinged out with flashing lights, advertising *Dream Girls, Annie, Legally Blonde: The Musical* and *Hairspray*, Diamond wondered, "Will I ever have the chance to see a Broadway show?" Seven years ago, she would have been wondering, "Will I ever be in a Broadway show?"

Diamond knew her mother had been saving up to take them out on the town to see *Dream Girls* and to a late night dinner at a place with tablecloths and linen napkins. Diamond had asked for that for her upcoming birthday. For her fifteenth birthday. Would there be a fifteenth?

Dream Girls was one of Diamond's all-time favorite movies— she'd watched it several times and knew every song by heart—and she couldn't wait to see it on the stage.

She'd also been looking forward to grabbing a bite at Docks Oyster Bar & Seafood Grill. On special occasions, her hip, rich twenty-five-year-old cousin Sadie, along with Sadie's reasonably handsome husband Jude, treated Diamond to the dish she loved the most . . . chilled shrimp cocktail with fries. Nothing that would set them back a lot, though they could well afford anything she ordered, but not the cheapest thing on the menu. Diamond adored Sadie and Jude. Sadie was a professional ballet dancer and Jude was a rock music promoter, and together they had the hippest, sweetest, most amazing life that Diamond could imagine—living in aloft, hanging out with musicians and actors, wearing cool clothes, traveling.

Diamond had tried to think about Sadie and Jude during the cab ride.

And about *Dream Girls.*

As they wound their way through Manhattan, Diamond saw the usual sights through her half-mast opened eyes—people scurrying off to work with newspapers tucked under their arms like Giants players protecting footballs, honking taxicabs weaving in and out of traffic, and street vendors on almost every corner setting up their Sabra hotdog and hot nut stands. Diamond usually loved the pulse of the city and the aromas filling the air from all the smiling, waving street vendors—a kaleidoscope of color and sound. Her stomach rumbled at the notion of food, and she shifted her thoughts to her favorite street vendor, Emilio. He always had a bag of hot sugar-coated almonds waiting for her, claiming she was his favorite customer.

She met Emilo seven years ago, on a trip to the hospital after hearing the dreaded words: lymphoblastic leukemia. Her mother had stopped at his vendor stand, and they'd struck up an instant friendship. Emilo came to visit Diamond in the hospital—at first because he was visiting someone else there and so stopped in her room, too. But he came again just for her, and they'd stopped at his stand on subsequent trips to the hospital for "follow ups."

She knew that Emilio really cared for her, and sometimes she would fantasize that he was her long-lost father, looking out for her like a guardian angel. He, too, was Puerto Rican. She'd mused on more than one occasion that perhaps he was hiding his true identity, being more than a street vendor—doing that only for fun—and having a ton of money tucked away somewhere for Diamond and her mom.

Perhaps he was waiting for the right time to spring the news of his real name and wealth. It was an entertaining thought . . . but not enough to entertain her today. Maybe she should have asked her mother to have the cabbie stop at Emilio's two blocks back. Maybe she should have told Emilio about the cancer returning. Maybe he'd visit her again.

Diamond had never met her real father and didn't know anything about him . . . other than that he and her mother divorced when she was a newborn and that his name was Larry. At a young age, Diamond had done the math that her mother was only a teenager when she became pregnant, and tales of her high school days painted Marsha as rebellious, curious, fun-loving . . . and she clammed up when it came to the subject of "Larry." Diamond pressed, of course, to the point that her mother turned pale and would leave the room.

Though Diamond was eternally curious, she always backed off when she spotted the sadness reflected in her mother's eyes. Diamond figured today, if she pressed the point again, her mother might cave and actually say more than a few sentences about Larry.

In fact, Diamond was just about to broach the subject again, but her mouth went instantly desert-dry. They pulled up to the main entrance of New York-Presbyterian Morgan Stanley Children's Hospital.

"I feel sick to my stomach, Mama." She felt worse than sick. She felt like she was going to die.

Would there be a fifteenth birthday?

"Hold my hand. It'll be okay. Before you know it, you'll be back to your ecstatically bubbly personality. You'll feel better than before. Everything will be fine."

If I live through it, Diamond thought. *Fine. Okay.*

After checking in through admissions, the hospital's Child Life Specialist, Jessica Cullen, escorted them to a vibrantly colored private room in the Child and Adolescent Oncology Unit.

O-n-c-o-l-o-g-y. That was another word Diamond could spell without thought.

Insurance certainly won't cover all of this.

"Make yourselves comfortable," Jessica said. She was blond, perky, and Diamond put her at a little younger than her mother. Jessica's smile looked genuine enough but, as Diamond studied her, she realized it didn't quite reach her eyes and guessed that it was a practiced expression.

Jessica kept talking, but Diamond was so preoccupied that she missed some of it. "Pardon," she said.

"I said if you need anything, let me know. I've heard you like music and movies, so I put a few CDs and DVDs on the stand. I thought you might enjoy them. Later, if you feel like it, we'll check out the teen room together and do some arts and crafts. Sound good?"

Diamond nodded and replied, "Cool. Thanks much. I'd like that." She didn't feel as cheery as her words sounded.

Marsha leaned over to Diamond and whispered in her ear, "Wow! I must be getting old. Jessica looks like she could be my daughter."

Old.

Diamond felt too old to be here.

"I'm getting old for this place, Mama. Look at the little pink and purple bunnies on the border trim." If she was seven—like the first go-round with this—she might have appreciated the décor. "This room ought to make you feel young again."

Marsha smiled and put on a brave face, and Diamond's lip quivered.

"Don't leave me, Mama," she said. As brave as she wanted to be—and told herself she needed to be—her stomach twisted at the thought of her mother leaving her each day to go to work.

And work was necessary. Diamond was old enough to have a better-than-vague comprehension about insurance and bills and how-much-would-they-owe-for-all-of-this, especially this being a private room. Diamond briefly considered telling her mother to cut back on costs and get her a room with multiple beds. But as quickly as that thought came, she pushed it aside; it was all right to be selfish at a time like this.

"Mama, don't leave. Promise me that you'll be right by my side—no matter what," Diamond urged. "Please don't leave me alone while I'm stuck in here!" Her mother had stayed by her seven years ago—all day long at first, then gradually slipping away for errands and work, but always making some sort of appearance before it was lights out.

"I told you Niña, you don't have to worry." Marsha's voice sounded reassuring to Diamond. "My boss, Al . . . you remember Al. He's letting me work from home for awhile or, in this case, from the hospital. He said that he never worked with a legal secretary who could type depositions as fast as me, so he doesn't want to lose me. So don't worry! My job is secure, even if I don't show up in person every day there for awhile."

For awhile. The words rattled around in Diamond's head. It would be like before—all day long at first, her mother would stick by her, and then she'd gradually slip away for longer periods and go back to work. She had to, all the bills that would be coming in. Insurance would never cover everything. Besides, why would her mother want to stay in a place like this? Sickness everywhere, the smell of disinfectant thick and cloyingly covered with something floral. Why should she expect her mother to suck in this air every minute of every day? Her mother wasn't the one with leukemia, after all.

Lymphoblastic leukemia. Cancer. Cancer. Cancer.

"Al would do anything to keep me working for him," Marsha continued. She'd been saying something else, but Diamond hadn't caught it. "Plus, you know how much he cares about you. You've gotta give your old lady a pat on the back for being such a superstar. So I can work from here for awhile. Understand?"

For awhile.

Marsha's further attempts to lighten the atmosphere fell on Diamond's deaf ears.

It didn't take long to settle in, and soon Marsha was on the phone with Al.

"*Quisiera que hubiera algo que pudiera hacer por Diamond. Se mira tan preocupada por todo,*" Marsha said into the cell, whispering in Spanish.

As if that would keep me from listening in to their conversation. Diamond, propped up in bed mentally translated: "I wish there was something I could do for Diamond. She looks very worried about everything." Diamond played with a laptop that Al had loaned her, letting her mom's conversation drift to the background.

The laptop was a great distraction, helping to tug her mind away from what was to come. She immediately Facebooked Shayna, who was hanging out with Tamara. All three agreed on a "cyber chat," though Shayna wondered why Diamond hadn't called to chat with real voices. *Because my voice will crack. Because I'll cry,* Diamond thought. *Because you're probably my very best friend and I already cried enough to you.* She didn't reply to Shayna's question and instead began typing a message about the cab ride, about the cracked vinyl seats and all the food vendors she saw on the way here. She even typed about the purple and pink bunnies that ringed her room.

Diamond became quickly attached to the new laptop and wondered if Al would ask for it back.

****

Shaynapunim:
wuz up girla it's your girls

LiDiamond:
i wish i knew WTF wuz happenin.

Shaynapunim:
hang in there girla

LiDiamond:
don't know wat I'd do without ya

Shaynapunim:
it's tamara.

LiDiamond:
hey

Shaynapunim:
just keep thinkin bout mr bad boy

Shaynapunim:
now i know you smilin

LiDiamond:
lol

LiDiamond:
wat a thought. i like i like. O! He'll never be
interested in me. i'll be the bald Nuyorican
cancer chick.

Shaynapunim:
don't say that.

LiDiamond:
whateva

LiDiamond:
gotta go

Shaynapunim:
4U

LiDiamond:
you

Shaynapunim:
how can we help

LiDiamond:
UR

Shaynapunim:
no prob we got your back girla

> **LiDiamond:**
> lol

> **Shaynapunim:**
> lol

> **LiDiamond:**
> bye

> **Shaynapunim:**
> bye

****

Marsha left early to run into the office and pick up some reports. The leaving her alone in this place had started already, Diamond thought. But maybe she wouldn't be gone long.

After a night of being poked and prodded by nurses—the endless needles hurt at fourteen as badly as they had seven years ago—Diamond was happy to see Jessica come bounding into the room bright and early in all her famous, perky glory. She was holding a brown plush teddy bear in one arm.

"I thought you might like this little dude to hold onto when you wake up. Wait a minute . . . that didn't sound right. I mean, you might like to have a stuffed animal when you come out of the anesthesia."

Diamond graciously chuckled, "I understand. You are *so* sweet. That teddy bear is the cutest!" She didn't mean it, but the words made Jessica smile. Diamond thought the teddy bear looked infantile, but it felt soft to her fingers. Would have been a far better gift had someone given it to her seven years ago. "Yeah, I'll have him when I come out."

Anesthesia. Diamond's lower lip trembled and Jessica noticed.

"C'mon, forget the bear. Let's go to the teen room and play some Pac-Man. How's that sound?"

"S'okay," Diamond said. "Cool, I guess." She feigned to brighten. "Good idea. Because of the . . . procedure . . . today, I haven't been able to eat. Nerves, you know, at first, and then 'cause they told me not to eat because of the . . . procedure. But I'm actually hungry enough to eat some Pac-Man dots!"

With the game beeping and blaring in the background (wah-wah-wah-wah-wah) in the well-lit room packed with arts and crafts, magazines, video gaming systems and a large flat screen television, Jessica asked: "Do you remember having the Broviac catheter or central line put in your chest last time?"

Diamond's lip quivered a little more. So the pleasantries of Pac-Man were meant as a diversion, something to soften the conversation about the medical stuff. *Suck it up,* Diamond scolded herself. *Jessica doesn't need to see you like this or she'll think you really are at the right level for the teddy bear.*

"The Broviac . . ." Jessica pressed, raising her voice a little over the game.

"Yeah, I remember." A pause. "I think I do."

"The catheter was surgically inserted and they gave you this general anesthesia to put out so you wouldn't feel anything. That's what we've scheduled for tomorrow. Same thing. Simple. Routine for something like this. And I promise you, it won't hurt a bit."

Yeah, right.

"Plus, I'll be with you dudes," Jessica added thoughtfully, pointing to the teddy bear as one of the team. Diamond had it tucked under her arm. "See, nothing to worry about."

Diamond pulled a face. "It's not the Broviac catheter I'm uptight about. It's what's gonna run through it that's freakin' me out." She was surprised she confided in Jessica and instantly cursed herself for doing so.

Jessica gently patted Diamond's arm. "Listen, I know you're scared about the chemo drugs and their side effects. I'll be honest with you—I think I'd be scared, too. You're taking all of this in like an adult, not like a kid. I've known people twice your age who were basket cases. But everyone has different responses to the treatment. Some don't even experience many side effects at all. Honest. And although others may feel sick, there are different ways to alleviate discomfort. So let's deal with one thing at a time. Everything will be okay."

Okay. Fine.

With a sigh, Diamond shrugged. "Awesome sauce. I guess."

The rest of the day rushed by, and after the half-hour surgery the next morning to insert the catheter, Diamond's mother and grandmother, Salma, were waiting for her to regain consciousness in the recovery area.

Diamond drifted in a current of incoherent babble while fighting off the effects of the anesthesia, the recovery taking longer than the actual procedure. A part of her realized she was chattering disjointedly, and she tried to vaguely sort through the mish-mash of words that tumbled unbidden from her lips. As the minutes passed, her ramblings became a little easier to understand. It was like she was dreaming while half-awake, and it felt like she was thinking things and not really aware she was sharing all of those thoughts with anyone within earshot.

"Oh, Adam! You're such a bad boy! Do you know I call you Mr. Bad Boy? The name's for a reason. Nobody would ever believe what we're doing, you and me. I mean, everyone thinks I'm such a Virgin Mary. I can't believe you like me. I've always liked you. Mmmmmm, that feels soooo good! I've never done this before. Kiss me again."

Salma gasped and, through hazy eyes, Diamond saw Marsha's face turned bright red. Soon, Spanish was rapidly flying between the two women, so fast Diamond had a hard time making it out, and couldn't tell which one of them was saying what.

"¡¿Virgen María?! Así es, Virgen María. ¡Escuchemos a la Virgen María! ¿Qué te hace sentir tan bien? ¡Esta es mi pequeña niña! ¡No puedo creer esto!"

A part of Diamond translated their conversation:

"The Virgin Mary?"

"Yes, the Virgin Mary."

"Let's listen to the Virgin Mary."

"What makes you feel so good?"

"This is my little girl! I can't believe this!"

Jessica entered the room, which brought the heated exchange to an end. She leaned over to Marsha and whispered loud enough for Diamond to hear: "Is Adam her boyfriend?"

"She's fourteen. She doesn't have a boyfriend," Marsha replied. "Not that I'm aware of. Fourteen year olds only *think* they have boyfriends. They have crushes. I knew she had a wild crush on some boy, this Adam probably, but that's all I knew about."

Jessica responded, "before you have a heart attack, don't jump to any conclusions. I've heard kids say weird stuff under anesthesia before. A lot weirder than that. She could be chattering about something from a movie or book."

Marsha lowered her voice and Diamond, still groggy, had to struggle to hear. "In my heart. In my heart I know she's not sexually active. She's a good girl, my Niña."

"Is she? I wonder." Salma tsk-tsked. "Such language."

Shortly before noon, Diamond was wheeled back to the bunny room, a lot less muzzy by now, and she fixed her gaze on a dozen yellow roses in a big glass vase at her bedside. She also found her two smiling cousins, Sadie and Jude, waiting for her. She was happy they'd taken the day off work to come visit.

"Cool! Yellow roses are fresh to death!" Diamond heard herself plainly, but she thought the words were a little muffled, like her tongue was still thick from the sedation. And "fresh to death." There was that eight-ton elephant hiding in the corner . . . the word death. Maybe no one heard her utter it. "Those are soooooo fresh! Thanks, you dudes."

"Of course they're fresh," Salma said. "Sadie got them downstairs in the—"

"Fresh means something a little different now," Sadie said.

Salma mumbled something about words being words and that the meaning of them shouldn't change through the years.

Diamond noticed that her cousins' faces were slightly flushed, like they'd been running or something, and she had the feeling that her cousins, along with Marsha and Salma, had been having some sort of party prior to her arrival. Dancing maybe. Jogging down the hall.

Sadie suddenly giggled and whispered something to Marsha. She then turned to Diamond and said in a mocking tone, "Oh, Adam! You're such a bad boy!"

Bamboozled, Diamond asked, "What the . . . what? What are you talkin' about?"

Hadn't she been dreaming about Adam? She had been dreaming about him and about calling him Mr. Bad Boy, and weren't they doing . . . things . . . in the dream? She certainly wouldn't actually talk about him to anyone but Shayna. How could Sadie know about Adam?

"Sadie," Diamond persisted. "What are you talkin' about?"

"That's what *we* want to know," Marsha interjected. "What are *you* talking about? What have you—who have you—been talking about nonstop since they wheeled you out? Who is Adam?"

Diamond tried to shake off the questions, looking away from them and following the route of the bunnies around the room. Had she been talking aloud about Adam? Had it been one of those waking dreams she'd read about in a magazine? *Please no,* she thought. *Please don't let me have talked about him so that they could hear.* They couldn't have been privy to her dream about Adam, could they? How embarrassing! How personal! How none-of-their-business! *How did they know about Adam?*

"Spill," Sadie said. "Who's this Adam?"

"I have no idea what *you're* talking about," she cut back, almost a little too harshly and quickly. Weird that Sadie would even mention Adam's name. "Adam?" She sucked in her lower lip. "Who's Adam?"

"That's what we really, really want to know." This from Salma. She added a finger wag for emphasis. "Too bad you came out of the anesthesia. It was getting interesting hearing about him."

Diamond felt the color flee from her face. "Adam," she started. "Well, there's an Adam in my class. Maybe . . ."

"And he must be a bad boy," Sadie and Jude said practically in unison.

"H-H-How do you know about . . ." Diamond pleaded with them to explain, and finally everybody clued her in on her incoherent anesthesia-induced conversation.

"I'm so embarrassed," Diamond whined when she finally, fully realized that she had unconsciously disclosed her most intimate desires to her mom and grandmother and cousins . . . and whatever perfect strangers had been in the recovery room. She was more than embarrassed, she was mad.

Amid the laughter and mocking, Marsha suddenly became serious and came close, her mouth against Diamond's ear.

"Niña, are you still a virgin?"

Do the math, Mom, she thought . . . she wanted to say. *You're thirty. I'm fourteen . . . not far from fifteen. That means you were pregnant when you were, oh, probably fifteen. Sexually active when you were fifteen. Maybe earlier. But, no, I'm not like you were. I'm not loose, and I'm not promiscuous. I'm not going to get pregnant. And I am going to finish high school.*

"Are you still a virgin?" she repeated.

If I was Nuyorican Knockout right now, I would bump my butt right out of here and fly through that window to escape all of this humiliation. I'd be indestructible, and my personal life would remain personal. My personal life should be personal!

But Diamond wasn't a flying superhero, and her mother was asking her a pretty important question.

She dropped her voice to a whisper, hoping only her mother would hear. "I never hooked up with Adam. He barely even notices me. It's sad, but true. I'll probably be a virgin until I'm twenty-two. And this is not the place to ask me something like that."

Marsha looked at the little Virgin Mary idol perched on the windowsill and said, "*Gracias a Dios.*"

Crestfallen, Diamond sputtered louder than she had intended, "What do you mean, 'thank God?'" The only person she could see right now was her mother. She forgot about her grandmother and her cousins, the nurse, and whoever else might be walking by in the hall. "Thank God? Don't you ever want me to live a normal life? I probably never had a chance with Adam in the first place, and now, who would ever be interested in me? Cancer girl? I'll be a virgin forever. I'll be a virgin until I . . . die."

There it was, another eight-ton elephant.

And just how many eight-ton elephants can fit in one hospital room? the fourteen-year-old cancer patient asked. *How many can pirouette in front of the yellow roses before someone notices them?*

Diamond's mind spun and the colors in the room intensified. The yellow roses and the purple and pink bunnies warred with her mother's red shirt and made her dizzy. She dropped her head hard into the pillow.

"Hey, hey, hey." Sadie was there, brushing her face. "What your mom means is you've got a lot on your plate right now, Dia. You're only fourteen and shouldn't be thinking about boys in that way. Don't grow up too quick, okay. Believe me, when the time is right, some years from now, you'll know, and you'll find the right person."

Diamond looked around Sadie, her eyes locking pleadingly onto Salma. "Abuela, do you believe in all this?"

Salma shuffled close and joined the crowd around Diamond's bed, shouldering her way in and giving Diamond a reassuring hug. "It's all right, baby," she whispered. "We're just having a little fun with you."

"Fun at my expense," Diamond grumbled. "Like I need that. I need a lot of things other than fun at my expense. I need . . ." *To be free of cancer. To be anyone but me. To be anywhere but here. To never hear the words lymphoblastic leukemia ever ever ever again.*

The colors had stopped spinning, and now the scents of the room were coming to the fore—the antiseptic, cleansers, the soft smell of the roses, and the sharp, too-sweet pong of Salma's cologne. Diamond fought to keep from gagging.

"You know, Mama, according to the way you dudes are treating me, I might as well have had sex already," Diamond pouted. *Maybe they were trying to keep the conversation on sex and Adam as a way to avoid talking about chemotherapy and cancer. Maybe they mean well.* "You ought to trust me." She nearly added: "I'm not having sex, and I'm not going to be a teenage mother like you were." But she swallowed those words and instead offered her mother a lopsided smile.

There were giggles all the way around, and her visitors backed off and gave her a little space.

Diamond then turned her attention to Sadie and Jude. Sadie in her Baby Phat-wearing glory and Jude with his tattooed ear pierced swagger made Diamond wish that she was hanging out in their Tribeca loft.

Sadie, always an expert at softening difficult subjects, said, "Do you remember when you saw me in my first performance with the New York City Ballet?"

Diamond's face lit up. "Yes! I felt like a princess!"

Sadie beamed. "You *are* a princess, and also such a sweet girl! You need to know that. And this Adam . . . whoever he is . . . will either like you because he'll see how special you are, or he'll miss having the best girlfriend ever because he's stupid. And if he's stupid, well, he's certainly not the right guy for you."

Diamond couldn't help but smile even wider at that.

"See, Niña, when you believe in yourself it shows. Make sure you let him see you shine . . . really sparkle . . . and you'll have nothing to worry about."

Diamond nodded. "Since you brought it up, how's the ballet business going?"

Sadie winked. "I'll tell you later. When it's just us."

Jude, who up to this point had been talking on his cell phone and missed the entire conversation, finished his call and made a show of clearing his throat. "Hey, Diamond! I'm promoting the new 40/40 Club. It's one of the hottest spots in New York City. When you start feeling better, Sadie and I were thinking we could give you your first nightclub experience, since you're so into the music scene. Hey, it pays to have a cool cousin with connections!"

Diamond laughed. "Fresh! When do you think we're gonna go?" Her voice got higher and higher as she got more excited. "Oh my God! This is amazing! What should I wear?"

Someone stopped outside her door and poked a head in,

curious. It was no one Diamond recognized, but they waved and then moved on.

"To wear?" Sadie said, "We'll figure that out. Something new, definitely. And that will require a shopping trip. My treat. And we'll post pictures on Instagram, too!"

"Girl, you bet. We'll have so much fun," Diamond responded.

Sadie stood directly in front of Diamond now, giving her a good look at the ultra hip outfit she was wearing. Diamond leaned forward so she could see the shoes, too.

"I really like your Pastry Sneakers, or should I say your fab Cookie Chocolate Wafer Pastry Kicks. I'm dying for a pair . . ."

They were nine-ton elephants now. Ten tons.

The conversation came to a sudden halt.

Dying. She'd said the "D" word again.

They were ten-ton elephants all pirouetting around the fresh-to-death yellow roses and everyone noticed them.

No one breathed.

The sounds of the hospital beyond this room crept in . . . a muted conversation, someone wheeling a tray down the hall, a buzzer going off, a boy calling "nurse!"

Dying.

The word was loaded like a gun held at point blank range to Diamond's head.

"Dying," she whispered. "Dying. Dying. Dying."

The elephants multiplied and twirled.

Sadie returned to the subject of shoes. "I'm glad you like them. They're mega-comfortable. I'll get you a pair next time we go shopping in the city. But you'll have to try them on. I'm lousy at guessing sizes. In fact, once for Jude's birthday, I—"

At that moment Jessica came into the bunny room with a Starlight Fun Center—a portable flat screen TV entertainment center—and with a few more DVDs and a Wii.

"Look what just became available," Jessica chirped. "I thought I'd snag it for you before someone else did. I hope you don't mind me barging in like this. You don't, do you?"

"I guess I could find a use for it," Diamond pretended to mope. Her ruse lasted only a heartbeat. "Majorly cool!" she squealed. "Thanks, Jessica. You're the best. I always wanted a Wii, but my mom said it was too expensive for us."

"They are expensive," Marsha said softly.

Jessica settled herself in the rocking chair and looked to the others in the room, softly drumming her fingers on her knee. Sadie and Jude made an exit, mumbling something about going in search of some sodas, and dragging Salma with them.

It took Diamond only a moment to realize Jessica had politely shooed her relatives out.

"I brought you something else, too," Jessica continued. "Since chemo affects patients differently, we don't know for certain if your hair will fall out."

Diamond's fingers drifted up to touch her head.

"So why not have fun with it while we can, huh?" Jessica pulled out a collection of hair dyes in every color imaginable from a sack she'd been toting. "What color tickles your fancy?"

With an impish smile, Diamond answered, "Um . . . blue. I think I'd like blue hair."

Jessica replied, "Great! Blue it is! But be prepared. If your hair doesn't fall out, you'll be really colorful."

Colorful would be better than bald, she thought. *Why did this have to happen to me?*

Jessica opened her mouth to say something else, but stopped and met Diamond's gaze. "Tired?"

Diamond was tired . . . from the after effects of the anesthesia, from all the company . . . tired because she'd gotten so very little sleep last night, tossing and worrying about today. She yawned. "How about we color it in a little while. Tomorrow?"

"Great." Jessica left the blue dye with Diamond and Marsha. "Tomorrow, I'll be back with more surprises. Get some rest. And we'll get to the blue soon enough."

Marsha got comfortable on the rollout couch next to the bed

and, though she closed her eyes, Diamond could tell she wasn't sleeping; she was keeping a watchful eye on her baby girl. Diamond watched her mother's lips move and picked up some of the words. She was praying.

Diamond prayed, too, that the chemo drugs would lead to a full recovery, that Nuyorican Knockout was real and would swoop in here and save her.

****

The next day was another big hurdle for Diamond, as she was beginning her high-dose chemotherapy.

To start things off, Jessica arrived early with a Jay-Z CD and placed it next to Diamond's laptop in full view.

"I thought Jay-Z's *Black Album* would be a good choice," Jessica announced. "I hope you like him."

"Thanks. I love it! I really dig Roc-A-Fella Records," Diamond replied.

Both Marsha and Jessica kept Diamond occupied through the morning by hanging out in the teen room to beat the high score on Pac-Man, surfing the channels between *Charmed* reruns and MTV, playing Wii on the Fun Center, and chowing down on Blue Bunny cherry popsicles.

That afternoon, Jessica helped Diamond dye her hair blue, and

Diamond was pleased to discover that she could actually pull off her fresh new look without looking like Smurfette.

"Girl, look at your hair! Wow, you're pretty, even in blue!" shrieked Taylor, the nurse on duty when she came in to get the chemo started. Decked out in Disney character scrubs, Taylor's bright white smile glowed against her rich cocoa complexion. And her musical Jamaican accent made her voice sound sweet and soothing. "Dr. Goldberg says we're ready to rock and roll with your chemo, so let's get you hooked up."

While the nasty chemicals dripped into Diamond's veins, she clung tightly to her teddy bear. For the next who-knew-how-many-weeks, this was going to be Diamond's life.

Facing the medicine and the weakness and gamely smiling for her mother and Jessica, pretending to be brave and hopeful . . . all of it was a tall order for a short Brooklyn girl with blue hair.

The Elephant Mambo

Nuyorican Knockout slipped out of Diamond's room, avoiding the janitor pushing a monstrous floor-buffer. It made a pleasant whirring sound Nuyorican found better than the "bleeps" and "hisses" of various pieces of equipment running in various rooms. On her swag surfer, she skimmed above the polished tile and shot down the corridor, the open and closed doors a blur, the nurses both in white and in colorful scrubs a rainbow swath that pulsed in time with a Jay-Z tune playing on the floor above and that Nuyorican could amplify with her hyper-hearing. She picked up the smell of cleaning products and various other things she couldn't put names to and, and finding them too biting,

she pushed them away and thought about fresh air.

And she was out in it a moment later, flying through an

open window that had somehow appeared and racing

up the side of the hospital, beyond its roof and toward

the clouds.

> *Maybe the cure for lymphoblastic leukemia*
>
> *wasn't in this hospital or New York City or anywhere on*
>
> *Earth. Maybe it was out there in the stars and it would*
>
> *be her task to find it and bring it back to save Diamond*
>
> *and all the others in the cancer wing.*

Diamond quickly but reluctantly settled into a hospital routine that she remembered all too well. She thought it odd that she couldn't recall a lot of things from her early childhood—favorite toys and first friends and the like, her first "A," her first and only trip to the principal's office, everything else all blurry and indistinct and relegated to some long-lost part of her brain. But she could remember vividly every aching detail about her previous hospital stay, like watching a rerun in high-def.

Every aching detail.

At times, she swore that she was about to wig out from all of it. She hated being weak and sick, and her mood flip-flopped constantly between frustration and hope. One minute, she thought she was dying and wondered what death would be like and the hereafter . . . and what if there wasn't a hereafter. The next minute, she was confident she'd beat this horrid disease into next Tuesday and be back to school in short order.

But often she was simply too tired to feel anything, so she just zoned out in bed for hours at a time while the world rolled on without her.

Diamond loved that her mother was there most of the time.

She also hated that her mother was there most of the time.

It was comforting to have her mother in the same room, even if she was hunched over a laptop typing away on whatever project her boss had set up.

But, in some respects, her mother's presence made her feel like a toddler, clinging and crying and . . . God why did she have to get this disease again?

Sometimes, she wanted to be alone and did everything but say aloud the words that thrummed through her head: "Mama, just leave for a while." *Let me be alone with my terrible, awful fear that's eating at my heart and head.*

Sometimes they laughed and joked together, sometimes they argued, and sometimes they just sat together in silence, Diamond drifting in and out of sleep and Marsha sitting in her chair staring out the window and face bathed softly in the light coming from the laptop screen.

Sometimes Diamond saw tears rolling down her mother's cheeks, and always she pretended that she didn't see them. Sometimes tears rolled down Diamond's cheeks too, and she tried to wipe them away before her mother saw.

It's just the smell of the cleaning products they just sloshed around in the hall and the bathroom . . . that nasty, sharp smell that brought tears to my eyes, Diamond thought. But it was the cancer that brought them several times every day.

As often as it was possible for them to travel into the city, Tamara and Shayna visited after school . . . it wasn't often enough. They'd come bounding into the bunny room, as Diamond called it, all full of excited gossip about their friends and, of course, all the latest news about Mr. Bad Boy Adam while whoever brought them waited patiently down in the lobby.

And one day they brought Diamond some way-cool Hello Kitty pajamas. She didn't have the heart to tell them they were a size too big . . . she'd lost some weight since checking in. Cancer did that. . . cancer and all the chemicals.

"Math sucked today," Tamara said. "Boring mostly. Not boring easy, just boring. Some of the problems were really hard, but not interesting. Could've taken a nap."

Shayna made a tsk-tsking sound and talked about what everyone was wearing.

Diamond shoved all the tales she didn't really care about to the background, focusing on the happy sounds of her friends' voices. In truth, she only wanted to hear about Mr. Bad Boy.

"He asked about you," Shayna announced.

Diamond's heart skipped a beat. "What did he say?"

Shayna shrugged and twisted the ball of her foot against the floor.

"He wondered where you were," Tamara supplied.

Diamond almost asked what they'd told him.

"What about the test we took?" Diamond changed the subject.

"We're in," Shayna said.

"To Hunter," Tamara added, her chin thrust out. "But they didn't post the results, on a bulletin board or nothing. It's all word of mouth who's in and who's not. That kind of stuff. They'll probably post everything later."

"Did anybody tell you how you did?" this from Shayna. "Not that you need to worry. I mean, if we got in, you got in. You probably aced them."

"I should have my mom call," Diamond said. "I just hadn't thought about doing that."

"We'd just die if you didn't go there with us," Tamara said.

Die.

The ten-ton elephants waltzed with the purple and pink bunnies that circled the room. Neither of her friends noticed.

"Yeah, we'd just die if you were stuck behind at old MS—" Shayna's voice trailed off.

The elephants were doing the mambo now and Shayna finally spotted them.

"Yeah, I'll have my mom call," Diamond said. The cheery visit had instantly soured. Would there be another year of school? Would there be another year of anything?

****

Sadie and Jude visited every few days, and they could always be counted on to bring awesome presents and piles of new CDs, along with an assortment of flowers. But it was usually bouncy, blonde Jessica who most helped Diamond through the endless hours.

"Got a surprise, girl!" Jessica said one rainy day. Marsha was out running errands. "Tattoos!"

"Get out! My mother'd string me up by my toenails!"

"Chill, Diamond. They're removable. Pick one you really dig. Let her freak out and you can pretend it's real."

Diamond loved that idea, and she picked a big, bold red heart, wishing it had the words "Adam loves Diamond" inscribed inside.

Jessica helped her apply it to the side of her right upper arm, where it would be clearly visible when her mother returned.

The plan worked. When Marsha came back and sat on the edge of the bed, Diamond could barely hold back her giggles. It didn't take Marsha more than a couple of heartbeats to react.

"You let her get a tattoo?" Marsha sputtered at Jessica, her red face glowing and eyes unblinking. "How could you do this, Jessica? How could you be so irresponsible? How did anyone get tattoo needles in here? I'm going to report you and . . ."

Diamond and Jessica both burst out laughing, which caused Marsha to stare from one to the other, the color slowly leaving her face and her mouth opening and closing like a captive goldfish.

"Figure it out yet, mom?" Diamond asked coyly.

Marsha started laughing, too.

The prank had been fun, but it tired Diamond out, and she had to lie back and close her eyes. *Weak as a kitten,* she thought, *one swallowed up by the voluminous material of the Hello Kitty pajamas.* Were the ten-ton elephants having a party?

She reached for her iPod and surrendered to the Kanye West music, and soon she was lost in his driving-beat world, surrounded by the images from his rap music videos. The elephants stepped in time to it, nimbly avoiding the purple and pink bunnies that cavorted around their massive feet. Then the music grew louder and the elephants melted away.

This is how Diamond passed her days and nights in the hospital. Conversation, music, shared gossip from school, rotating bouquets of flowers that kept at bay the bulk of the disinfectant smells.

She was often nauseous, and she had now begun to lose her hair. Before all of it fell out, she and Jessica dyed it deep purple, then red, then pale green.

Until there was nothing left to color.

"This is creepin' me out," and "I'm screwed," were Diamond's constant complaints. But Jessica cheered her up with a selection of colorful kerchiefs to cover her bald head.

Finally, after four weeks, the treatment was over and she was allowed to go home.

But was she cancer free, she wondered?

Were the elephants coming back to the tiny apartment with her?

Trey

Diamond was propped up in the back seat of a cab.

"Gotta stop at Emilio's." Jessica poked her head in the back window. "Don't forget. Emilio's."

He'd come by to visit twice during her four-week stay, neither time bringing her anything from his stand.

The thought of turning the tables and instead visiting Emilio quickly brightened Diamond's sagging spirits. She often imagined that her father might look and act like Emilio, which made being with Emilio almost like having her father there with her.

"I've got your back, corazón," her father said in her imagination. He spoke with Emilio's accent.

"I know you do, Papa," she mentally replied.

But her father—whatever he really looked and sounded like—soon faded away. So she listened to HOT 97 on the radio. They were playing "The Monster" by Eminem, featuring Rihanna. Eminem's tight bars seemed to spill into Diamond's heart.

And although Emilio's stand was operating, he wasn't there today, and the boy serving all his tasty specialties just shrugged when Diamond asked where he was.

"Shopping. Busy," the boy said. "Dunno. You want to buy something?"

"Just tell him Diamond says 'hi,' 'k?"

The music changed, the station still old, the cabbie favoring Neil Diamond and Barry Manilow, out-of-date geezers compared to the hip tunesters Diamond favored. Still, she managed to find some pieces to hum along to.

I love to sing, she reminded herself as she watched Manhattan fade into the distance, imagining her big booty Nuyorican super girl flying over the skyline, making everything okay again.

****

Back at the Lopez apartment, Diamond felt better.

She was really, really, really out of the hospital. And it didn't feel like the elephants had hitched a ride in the cab.

She hurried to her room, where J.Lo and Kanye beamed down

from the posters on the walls, welcoming her home. She glanced into the mirror and found herself staring at a too-thin girl with a big booty. "Shake that booty, girl!" she told herself, but her enthusiasm was less than enthusiastic. She danced only a few steps before collapsing on the bed, trying to catch her breath.

At least it's my own bed. But I sure don't feel like a Nuyorican big booty superhero anymore. In fact, Nuyorican Knockout hadn't made many appearances lately.

Even though the treatment was over and she was safe in her neighborhood, close to her friends and her extensive collection of Roc-A-Fella Records, her face was soon soggy with tears. Diamond listened to "Drive Slow" by Kanye West on her stereo.

Would driving ever be possible? Would she turn sixteen and get a license? Not that her mother had a car she could practice with . . . but that was a technicality. Would she hit the magic number that let her sign up for driver's ed? And would she get to take it in a good school? She'd never had her mother ask about the test. Would she claw her way out of the bottom-of-the-barrel school?

Drive slow, Kanye continued to croon.

Even without a car, without a license, driving slow wasn't an option for her. If anything, she'd been forced into the fast lane without any seat belts or airbags. She had so much on her itinerary, but not enough time to do it all. Follow-up doctor visits, school work, elephants to contemplate and keep at bay, hair to grow back.

"I'm so fugley! Adam will neva be interested in me," she grumbled. "What dude would be? I wanna be a 'somebody' and not another 'wanna be.' My life needs to make a difference and count for something! I don't wanna feel invisible anymore. And I don't want to be cancer girl."

Diamond's *Sexy Can I* ring tone interrupted her thoughts. Tamara was text messaging her on her cell phone.

CUtamara:
welcome home

LiDiamond:
hey

CUtamara:
u alright

LiDiamond:
idk chemo changed this girl's life

CUtamara:
got somethin that'll make you smile

LiDiamond:
what's dat

CUtamara:
shayna and i are comin to your crib to give u a makeover and hang tomorrow.

CUtamara:
it'll be bomb.

LiDiamond:
idk

CUtamara:
y

LiDiamond:
i cant do eeeeeeet. i look yucky. have you seen my fuzzy head? last time i looked like this i was 2 years old but I was cute then. i thought it'd be cool to be blue but it's jus weird. i'm a skinny blue loser.

CUtamara:
wat girl, u look fine. u be too hard on yo self. it'll be da 3 fem musketeers, me u and Shayna

LiDiamond:
lol

CUtamara:
don't punk out on us.

LiDiamond:
giggle

Tamara:
lol

LiDiamond:
bye

Tamara:
see u saturday round 11in da mornin

The idea of her best friends seeing her with fuzzy baby hair didn't make her feel any better. In fact, it just made her cry even more, and Marsha apparently heard her weeping through their thin apartment walls.

She knocked on her daughter's door and asked, "Baby, are you okay in there? Can I come in?" She didn't wait for a reply, just opened the door.

Diamond screeched, "Mom! I need some space. And I'm not a baby anymore. Don't you get it? Babies don't have to deal with this stuff. I have NO privacy."

Marsha put on a sympathetic face. "I understand being sick is terrible. Being a tween can be difficult enough. And being both can be overwhelming. However, you still need to remember that you're talking to your mother, who ecstatically loves you no matter what. You're not the only one going through this. It's hard to watch you suffer."

Unchecked, Diamond continued her rampage. "You're not feeling me! Everything's up in the air! I don't know what's going to happen to me! Leukemia has changed my freakin' life!"

"Yes, it has. But it doesn't have to change YOU," her mom responded.

"Bull. It already *did* change me. Look at me! How am I supposed to go hang with Tamara and Shayna and act like everything's the same when it's *not?* I don't feel or even look the same way I did. Look at my hair . . . what I have of it. A peach has more fuzz than I do. Look at me!" She thrust out her skinny arm, the wrist bone protruding. "Are you looking?"

From out on the street a car horn sounded long and loud. There were shouts, two men getting into an argument. The horn sounded again and a door slammed, then tires squealed and things were quiet again.

"Yes, I'm looking."

"What do you see?" There was a challenge in Diamond's voice.

"I see something pretty special. You will always be Diamond Lopez no matter how you look. Do your thing!"

Diamond gave up trying to make her mom understand.

"Whateva."

"You need to rest up today, baby girl. Please don't get an attitude with me first thing. You're out of the hospital, but this is still going to be a long haul for both of us."

"Whateva."

"And don't take that tone."

"Yeah, well it's a particularly long haul for one of us, the bald one who's always throwing up her guts."

"You passed the test at school," Marsha said. "Just in case you were curious." She gently hugged her daughter and left the room.

Diamond turned on her iPod to listen to what she considered to be her theme song, "Can't Knock The Hustle." She adored Jay-Z lyrics; they made her feel invincible. They also made her realize she was being downright nasty with her mother. What gave her the right? Cancer? The disease didn't give her permission to use her mother as a verbal punching bag. She decided to apologize the next time her mother poked her head in the room.

"Passed the test," she said, thumbs playing over the iPod's slick surface. "So I can get out of the bottom of the barrel. That's if I live long enough."

****

At dinner, Diamond took only two bites of her mother's special meatloaf, the recipe she usually gobbled up.

"Don't have an appetite," she said by way of explanation.

"Well, try to eat a little more. I went to a lot of trouble making your favorite dish. And you have to keep your strength up."

"Did I *ask* you to make meatloaf? I don't think so! You should know I'm hardly able to eat anything."

They glared at each other. Both looked away quickly, and Diamond drank from her Dr. Pepper. They didn't say another word to each other all evening. Now she'd have to apologize again . . . when she calmed down.

****

Diamond fell asleep lying on the couch watching reruns on *Nick at Nite*. Marsha sat silently across the room, watching Diamond toss and turn.

****

The following week Diamond was wired for school. "Got my game face on. I can do it. No problem," she assured herself as she walked down the familiar hallways, even though she had a little trouble breathing. All the walking was tiring, as if the subway hadn't been fatiguing enough.

Were people staring at her? Oh, God, they were!

At that moment, Shayna and Tamara appeared, each one taking up a position at her side.

"Like old times!" Diamond trumpeted. She tried to make it sound like old times, even if she didn't have the same feeling behind the words. Put on her "game face" for her friends.

"Yeah, girl, welcome back!" Shayna nudged her shoulder.

There were hugs all the way around and suddenly the three were talking at once, gossiping about everybody at school, pointing at clothes, humming lines from favorite songs.

"Heard she's hooked up with an older dude!" This from Shayna.

"No way! Not her!" Diamond shook her head and stuck out her chin.

"Way!" Tamara added. "Yes indeed way way way way waywaywaywayway!"

But during their chatter, Diamond noticed that Tamara and Shayna couldn't help but steal looks at the obvious wig that covered Diamond's bald head. She'd opted for a wig instead of scarves, and they'd found one that was close to her original color. But it wasn't quite the same, and they didn't have a big budget to work with . . . not the kind of money that would let her have real-looking tresses like the movie stars or Beyoncé or Shakira. It wasn't a bad-looking wig, but it looked like a wig.

Diamond's spirits went farther south with every glance Shayna and Tamara gave the wig. The strength left her legs, her stomach churned, and her heart skipped a few beats.

She was cancer girl again, and she'd brought a mamboing elephant to school with her.

Diamond, can you spell it . . . l-y-m-p-h-o-b-l-a-s-t-i-c l-e-u-k-e-m-i-a. Go to the head of the class! Why don't you wear a bright, white T-shirt with a honkin' big C on the chest.

Every subject dragged.

And sucked.

Diamond couldn't concentrate, her fingers reaching up to twirl the wig's hair.

In math, she saw Adam, Mr. Bad Boy, baggy pants, hottie, for the first time. *Really* saw him. Those sensitive hazel eyes were looking straight toward her. And a moment later they were doing a double-take at her wig.

Diamond looked away quickly.

I'm such a wuss with boys. I'm the cancer poster girl. Be careful

Adam, don't want you to get too close. Might get some cancer on you.

Oddly, she found herself missing the hospital and Jessica's sweet smile, so bubbly and perky. Jessica had tried to make Diamond happy . . . make her feel normal. Jessica wouldn't have done a double-take on the wig. Well, she might have volunteered to help Diamond color it blue.

Math finally ended, and despite her relief, Diamond was almost too weak to walk into the hall. She gasped for breath a couple times. More stares. It was hard to concentrate on breathing, trying to hide it as she hung with her friends.

"Mr. Bad Boy seems so into you, girl! Did you see the way he was always watching you? He whispers about you. You're such a *chicka*."

"Hot Hispanic girl?" Diamond translated. "I'm not hot."

"Hot you are. I told you he'd been asking about you. Yeah, he was so scopin' you out."

"Me? He was scopin' out my wig, dudes. I doubt he's all that into me."

Just then Diamond flinched as she heard the sickeningly nasal voice of Adora, the school "mean girl," coming up behind her.

"Well, look who came back from Cancerville! Contagious? You oughta wear a bell to warn people you're coming." Her army of skanks laughed.

"Back off, Adora," Shayna snarled.

"Wouldn't want to get any closer to whatever's under that nasty lookin' wig."

"Back off," Tamara said louder.

Adora turned to her cronies. "GTL time bitches," she said, and then snapped her manicured fingers.

The girls replied in unison, "We hear ya girl." The gruesome quartet sashayed away . . . three blond skanks and Adora with her own big booty, which was way too prominent on her short legs.

At that moment, the sky darkened and the Earth began to quake, because Nuyorican Knockout was approaching, swaying that awesome booty as she stomped through the school headed straight for the evil Adora. She'd been traveling the spaceways in search of a cure for cancer, and coming up empty handed decided to return and bail out Diamond.

Her heavy footsteps rattled the windows and the side-to-side motion of her powerful butt knocked down walls as she marched on until she was face-to-face with the now-terrified bully. With one mighty movement of her hips, Nuyorican Knockout smacked Adora down the hall, out the door, and into hyperspace!

****

At lunch, Diamond had to run from the cafeteria to the bathroom. Later, she tried to joke about it. "That mystery meat would make anyone want to barf."

Lame joke, Diamond, she told herself.

But her friends politely laughed at it and proceeded to guess just what the cooks put in the mystery meat.

When her afternoon history class ended, Diamond had to sit at her desk for several minutes fighting for breath before she could drag herself into the hall. And by the time her next class after that was over, she was wheezing, gasping and fighting for breath, unable to stand and unable to hide her discomfort.

"My asthma!" she said to no one in particular. "Oh, please, no!" She didn't have asthma, but it sounded better than "my cancer."

The next few hours were a blur.

She didn't say another word until she had been admitted back into the hospital. It had all happened so quickly, because her airway was so clogged that there might as well have been a big wad of wet rags stuck down it.

****

Her new hospital room had only pink bunnies on the walls, not a purple one in sight. But when Diamond tried to think of a funny bunny comment, she couldn't. Her efforts simply to breathe had exhausted her. There were no flowers . . . no one had time to buy them yet, and so she had to deal with that cloying odor of cleaning products that was overshadowed by something sweet—maybe one of the nurses had dabbed on too much cheap cologne.

As always, she was stabbed, jabbed, poked, prodded, and fussed over until she nearly freaked out. But, in a weird way, she kinda dug being safe and fussed over in the hospital again . . . kinda. At least here no one stared goofily at her wig. No one seemed afraid to touch her, and though she was "cancer girl," they didn't make her *feel* like she was "cancer girl."

Diamond was sore and weary, way sick of hacking and coughing and struggling for breath. And she was *waaay* bored. She always counted on the music from her iPod to take her from the real world to some cool, far out place where she really felt like herself. . . or, more to the point, felt like anyone but herself. But on this cloudy, weary day, even her music deserted her. By late in the afternoon, she was counting the pink bunnies.

Get a grip, girl! Get you . . . a hacking spasm interrupted her thoughts.

She lay back, exhausted, her ribs aching and weak as a. . .

bunny? *Not even close to clever, Diamond. Besides, bunnies are stronger than you.*

Was she going to lie there like this forever?

Why wasn't her mother back from the hospital office?

Where were her buds?

What was . . .

There was a noise intruding over the music. Someone else was coming in. "No!" She pulled the ear buds out. "No." She wasn't going to let one more person poke or jab her. Stubbornly, she kept her eyes closed, hoping that would make the intruder disappear. But then she sensed someone was hovering over the bed. Diamond inhaled a familiar scent. It was perfume... lilacs?

"Jessica!" Diamond opened her eyes and stared up at a smiling face with sparkling blue eyes. "Oh, I'm so glad to see you!"

They hugged. Diamond bit her lips together to not make a sound so Jessica wouldn't know that the hug was hurting her.

"Just couldn't stay away, huh, girl?"

"I missed the bunnies."

"Yeah, you can't have too many bunnies in your life."

They talked a little, dished a little, and then Jessica pulled out a Kanye West CD.

"This was just released. Not even in the stores yet from what I understand."

"Oh, Jessica, you're the bomb."

"Listen to the new disk, and soon you'll get a visit from a respiratory specialist."

"I'm sick of being stabbed and poked."

"Not to worry. No poking or jabbing involved. You'll actually enjoy his visit."

"Enjoy?"

"No, not going to say why. Let it be a surprise."

Jessica left, and Diamond slid Kanye West into the hospital's portable CD player. She closed her eyes again, drifting into the music's spell. She imagined that Adam was there with her, kissing her.

Then something pulled her back to wack reality. Someone else was at the side of the bed now. There was no lilac smell this time. Bummer. She hesitated, and then slowly opened her eyes to see staring back at her the dark eyes of a drop-dead gorgeous African-American man who was too beautiful to be real.

He might've stepped right out of her fantasy music world. She understood in a heartbeat why Jessica said she was going to enjoy the visit.

"Hi, I'm Trey and I'll be helping you breathe better. You're Diamond?"

"Diamond Lopez. Pleased to meet you." *Oh, God, what a lame thing to say, pleased to meet you. Sitcoms have better dialog than that.*

Even bad sitcoms.

"Now, you relax and just listen to your music."

"Yes . . ."

"Trey. My name's Trey."

"Yes, Trey."

Kanye West and this gorgeous man were both right in her face, and Diamond was suddenly happy. But Trey was handsome and she was a mess, the dark hair of her wig just buggin.' Why hadn't Jessica warned her about Trey, maybe the hottest dude she'd ever seen? Such swagger!

After she breathed deeply in and out of the nebulizer inhaler, Trey asked, "Is this helping you, Diamond?"

"Way helping, Trey." She didn't want it to end, didn't want him to leave. She felt tongue-tied, and then was afraid she'd say something dumb.

"I've got this dude at school . . ." She wanted to die, to pull the cover up over her head and cry her eyes quietly out. *Why am I telling him this?*

"Yeah? What's his name?"

"Adam. He's not really a boyfriend. Exactly. I mean, I'd be way willing . . ." Was her face warm? She'd die if she was blushing. Die . . . there was that wonderful word again. Bring on the elephants doing the mambo. "I don't think he notices me all that much."

"Then he's an idiot, Diamond."

"Yeah? You think so? Do you think I'm . . . pretty?"

"Diamond, you're a real cute girl."

Okay, girl, what would Nuyorican Knockout do now? Think! Think! I need some booty power just about now.

"Cute, yeah, I'll give you that. But do you think I'm pretty? There's a difference."

Why was he hesitating? Oh, God, why did I even ask him? He's a stranger. He's a stranger and I just told him all about Mr. Bad Boy.

"Of course you're pretty, Diamond. Dudes must go crazy over your dark eyes."

"You think so? Do you really . . ." *Chill, girl.*

"Well, I'll see you tomorrow and . . ."

"Adam's never kissed me, Trey. I know I'm only fourteen, and my mom would have a fit if she knew I was talking about this." Her cheeks were way burning. They must have been scarlet. "But I have friends a year younger than me, and they've kissed . . ."

"Never kissed you? That's too bad. But I'm sure when the time's right, some boy will kiss you. Once you're back at school."

Will I ever get back to school? "Would you kiss me, Trey?"

Trey squirmed, obviously uncomfortable. "I'm sure any boy would like that, but it's not professional. I could lose my job."

I could lose my life, Diamond thought. *And I certainly just lost my self-respect, spilling all this stuff to Trey. God, I'm so stupid.*

Trey looked away, and then looked down at the floor. Finally, he walked away.

I'm so stupid! Diamond began to cry. Her eyes closed in total defeat while she heard the gentle click of the door to her room shut. *How could I humiliate myself like this? I'll never be able show my face around this hospital again. At least he's gone now.*

But a moment later, she had a shock. Trey hadn't left the room after all . . . he'd just gone over to the door and closed it! His dark hands tenderly wiped the tears from her face. Then his face moved toward hers. She held her breath in anticipation.

Her whole body was throbbing. Boom, boom, boom! Was that her heart beating? It sounded like a drum pounding in her ears. Closer and closer, she could feel his body heat radiating against her skin. The smell of his cologne was intoxicating. His lips softly touched hers. She wanted this moment to last. Then, Trey slowly stood up and he was gone.

****

How much of the cancer was left inside her? How much had the chemotherapy killed? She envisioned it in patches and wished she could reach right inside herself and yank it out, be Nuyorican Knockout and booty-blast it into the next universe. Booty blast all the cancer in the whole world into the next universe so no one would ever get cancer again, never get hurt by it, never die by it, never lose their hair and miss school, never be stared at like you were leukemia girl.

So that no one would ever have to spell l-y-m-p-h-o-b-l-a-s-t-i-c l-e-u-k-e-m-i-a ever again.

Diamond closed her eyes with Kanye West still echoing in her ears. In her music-clad fantasy, it wasn't Trey, but Adam who held and kissed her passionately under the boardwalk with only the sounds of the waves crashing onto the shoreline and the clatter of trains in the distance.

It just doesn't get better than this. I never knew it could be like that, just a kiss.

Someone else was at the bed now. Jessica?

"Oh, it's you, Mama!"

"You seem to be breathing easier."

"I am. This therapist helped my breathing, and he . . ."

"You're blushing, Diamond. Is something wrong?"

"No, Mama, I feel better. It's just that . . ." No way could she tell her mother about the kiss. "I was just thinking a little about, well, you know, what's going to happen to me. I mean, does anyone really know? Have the doctors talked to you?"

"Diamond, we're going to think only ecstatically positive thoughts. I'm glad you're feeling better. Try to relax and just keep listening to your music."

"Actually, I don't feel that good. I'm nauseated."

"I thought we'd go down to the teen room for a purple Blue Bunny . . ."

"Mama, I said I'm nauseated. Aren't you even listening?"

Marsha stared at Diamond. "You just told me you were feeling better."

Diamond's eyes had lost their sparkle. "Yeah, well, I'm not. Not really."

"Okay, baby girl, I'll let you listen to your music and get some rest."

Diamond doubted her mother felt all that good either, the way she'd been hunched over her laptop trying to work. She smelled like coffee, which Diamond knew she'd been drinking a lot of.

"I'm going to the cafeteria," Marsha said.

Probably to get more coffee.

Diamond watched her mother walk slowly from the room.

So I'm stupid AND selfish. She sensed the toll this was taking on her mom. But it wasn't her fault! Diamond knew her mother's suffering was nothing compared to hers. *I've a right to be selfish. Not stupid, but selfish. Lymphoblastic leukemia gives me that right. It just doesn't give me the right to be so blasted rude to her. Dear God, how many times am I gonna have to apologize before this is all over.*

Diamond closed her eyes and tried to relax. Kanye's music took her away to a dreamy place where she could be someone else and with someone else. Again, she imagined her father.

"Oh, Papa, I'm way glad you're here! I've missed you so much. I didn't know if you'd ever come back."

"I'd never desert you, corazón. You're my Diamond. Hey, I named you that."

"I know you did, Papa, and I so love that name. What made you decide on Diamond?"

"It was a song by The Beatles, corazón: Lucy in the Sky with Diamonds. That was one of my favorites, back in the day."

"Did you like to dance, Papa?"

"You bet, corazón. I'm a dancing fool. Just like you. That comes from me, your dancing. Your mama, she's not so much with dancing."

"Don't I know it? Can we go dancing sometime, Papa? Just the two of us? Real soon?"

"Name the time, corazón. I know this cool place in Manhattan called the 40/40 Club."

The music ended.

"Bummer!"

Diamond shuffled through her CDs to find some Beatles tunes, looking for "Lucy in the Sky with Diamonds."

"Papa, I'm back and I'm so wired about. . ."

But her father had vanished.

"Papa, please come back."

Silence.

Diamond sniffled back tears and tried to visualize her father's face, seeing only the image of Emilio.

I don't know what he looks like! My own father! Was he dark-haired? Did he have dark eyes? Mama, I hate you for never telling me anything about him! My memories are all imagined.

What would people remember about her when she died?

Everyone died. Diamond just thought she might die soon.

Would they even remember what she looked like?

And just who would remember her?

Her mother?

Grandmother?

They'd kind of have to, she supposed. What about people who didn't have to? Like Shayna and Tamara? And Adam?

Yeah, right, I bet Adam's already forgotten me. If he ever knew I existed. Beyond seeing leukemia girl. And what about . . .

"Dudes! I'm so glad to see you! I was about to freak out! I'm so lonely here!" She wasn't, not with Albuela's overly-constant company, but she was glad to see Shayna and Tamara nonetheless, and thankful that someone had been willing to bring them into the city.

Her friends were full of hugs, smiles and—as usual—gossip about school and the people in the neighborhood. Diamond joined in eagerly.

"That little dweeb? Not even in a parallel universe!"

"He so did! Right there in the stairwell!" This from Shayna, who strutted back and forth at the end of the bed. "Right where the world could see him."

Diamond admitted that she felt better by the time they left, and they hadn't been gone more than a couple of minutes when Jessica bounced into the room. Half an hour in the teen room left Diamond in a much better mood, but exhausted.

"All the kids who come here—when they leave for good—do you ever remember any of them for long?" Diamond asked her. "I mean, like the ones who, you know, die? Do you remember them?"

The smile fled from Jessica's face. "Diamond, I remember all of my special friends. They become a part of me. YOU are such an important part of my life and YOU are a part of me, too! However, I really think you're going to walk out of here cured. I have every confidence that you're going to be cured. Then the question will be— will *you* remember *me?* "

"Don't blow me off, Jessica. I thought you were my special friend."

"I'm not blowing you off." Jessica sat on the bed. She held Diamond's hands as the young girl once more inhaled her sweet, cloying lilac perfume. "I mean it when I say that you *are* my special friend, Diamond. And I know that it's terribly important to have a good outlook on all of this, positive thinking heals, you know. So, look, for now I've got to check on a couple of other patients –but tomorrow, we'll have a long talk about this. Okay?"

"Okay. I guess."

Diamond watched Jessica walk out of the room, leaving her alone . . . like her mother had left her alone when she went to the cafeteria for more coffee. And where was her mom, anyway? Had she driven her away with her cross words and bad attitude?

"I'm sorry, Mom," she said, practicing another apology. "I am really, really, really sorry."

She wished Jessica hadn't mentioned looking in on other patients. She knew Jessica wasn't hers alone, but it had seemed like it. The notion made her feel warm and loved, especially when Jessica called Diamond her special friend. Diamond wondered if Jessica was taking other kids down to the teen room, laughing with them while they probably put on tattoos and dyed their hair blue and green and purple. Then talking them through chemotherapy, holding their hands when they got nauseated.

I want to die and get all of this over with.

The strangest feeling swept over Diamond, leaving her weaker and with a new kind of nausea, as though sour oatmeal was roiling around in her stomach and wanting to come right up to her throat.

No, I didn't mean that. Please, I don't really want to die!

She was sweating. Gross. She felt icky and sticky and panicked and hopeless all at once. And she didn't want to be alone one more minute. She reached around for the nurse call button.

Hesitated.

No! I'm not a wuss! I'm a big-booty Nuyorican superhero!

She coughed, her shoulders bouncing against the pillow. Then she laughed.

Yeah, sure, Nuyorican superhero, that's me.

Diamond was picking up her iPod when she realized her mother had come into the room. "Hi, Mama. Where've you been?"

My voice! Is that how I really sound? I sound so weak!

"The cafeteria. Their coffee is incredibly bad. I would say it's time to change the dirty sock in the coffee urn."

Diamond pictured a stinky old gym sock floating in the coffee.

"I just finished talking to Dr. Goldberg."

Diamond sat up straighter. "Good news or bad? Tell me quick. And tell me straight."

This was the first smile Diamond had seen on her mother's face in a few days.

"Baby girl, I can take you home."

Diamond had to catch her breath. "Home? Oh, Mama!" She'd been so certain she was going to be here for days, what with Trey coming to help with her breathing, saying he'd see her tomorrow.

They hugged for a long time. "This afternoon, baby, we're

going home."

Diamond pulled away. "Mama, I'm so happy that I'll be back in my own room. No more being poked and jabbed. And school again!"

"Afraid not on that count. You're not strong enough yet. The school is sending a tutor as part of a program called 'Home and Hospital.' We pushed you too soon sending you back when we did. Probably wouldn't have ended up back here if we'd taken it easy. You just seemed so full of energy and so wanted to go back."

Diamond pulled a face. "Tutor? Oh. For how long?"

"As long as it takes to get your strength back. You know, you could even go and stay with Abuela for a while. The tutor could go there. I called her after I spoke to the doctor, and her arthritis is much better now. She'd love to have you."

"But I want to go with home with *you*. Why do you want me to leave you? Did I do something wrong?"

There was a clatter in the hall; Diamond recognized the sound. Someone had dropped a tray. It was followed by a mumbled curse, an apology, and the hum of a vacuum cleaner.

"You did nothing wrong, baby. It's because I have to go back to work in the office. The boss says I have to be there now. But Abuela can look after you all day. We'll have dinner together every night. And Abuela is a much better cook than I am, but you know that."

"Jennifer Lopez was born in the South Bronx where Abuela

lives. So . . . ya! That'd be way cool." Diamond didn't really mean
that it would be way cool. She loved Abuela, and enjoyed visits to her
place, but it wasn't home. There was something comforting about being
in her own room with all of her things around her, the sounds of the
neighborhood coming in through the window—the arguments, car door
slams, occasional siren, dogs barking, clackity-clack of the train. All
of that was a music she was used to. But she knew all of this had been
difficult on her mother, and that her mother really did have to work.

Again, Diamond wondered how much of this insurance would
pay for. Not everything. She'd heard someone talking out in the hall
about a bag of chemotherapy drugs running around fourteen hundred
dollars. She wondered if her drugs had been that expensive. How many
bags had she had? How much savings did her mother have? And was
Diamond's illness going to siphon it all away.

"I'd love to stay with Abuela," Diamond said. She tried to put
enthusiasm into the words.

"You should start getting ready, Diamond."

"Right away, Mama."

When Marsha left the room, Diamond played the *Rent*
soundtrack… good music to pack by. She stood, but had to step back
and hold onto the bed. She was way weak. *Take it easy, girl. Chill for a
couple of minutes.*

It was then she realized her mother hadn't said just what the doctor had said beyond the fact that she could go home.

The song playing was "Without You." At that moment, she started to cry. Originally, she believed that the movie and, for that matter the Broadway show, was self-indulgent. But now, as Diamond leaned against the bed and held her stuffed bear, she could understand why most of the songs started tears streaming down her face.

Maybe the doctor said she could go home because there was nothing else the hospital could do for her. She was beyond hope. The cancer was going to win. That eighty percent that had shrunk to twenty percent was now zero percent.

What happens if I die? When everyone else's life goes on, will anyone take time to remember me for five minutes? Will they think of me? What comes after life? Is there anything? Is it all a big, black nothing? Was all of this . . . life . . . for nothing?

She wiped her face with the back of her hand. Slowly, she steadied herself, and walked to the closet with careful baby steps.

"We're getting out of here," she told the stuffed bear, still a favorite and well-loved player of hers. "We're going to Abuela's!" A Beyoncé song was made for this sort of thing, and so she switched out the CD. The music revved her spirits and made packing easier.

525,600 Minutes

Diamond sat on the couch and watched MTV. Salma handed her a can of guava juice.

"Abuela, doesn't guava juice make you feel like you're surrounded by palm trees? That's how it makes me feel."

"Niña, you make me smile. I think I'm going to have to drink more of that nectar. I would like very much to be surrounded by palm trees."

Diamond nursed the guava nectar, holding it on her tongue and letting it fill her senses. It was all she could smell, too, which she thought an improvement on the room air freshener her grandmother habitually had displayed on the coffee table. The air freshener was one of those plastic varieties that the Dollar Store sold, and this one was labeled "morning rain," though it smelled more like pine. There was another one like it in the bathroom, and one with a different fragrance on the windowsill in the kitchen. Diamond knew there were at least a dozen more of them in the pantry closet, French vanilla, pumpkin pie spice, cranberry, and more. Her grandmother liked to stock up when they were on sale.

Salma sat next to her and asked about the latest hospital visit.

Diamond turned down the volume and patiently answered each question. Well, as patiently as she could. Mostly, she wanted to forget the whole thing.

"Do you want more guava, Diamond?"

"Yes, thank you, but I can get it."

"No dear, save your strength."

Salma stood, smiled at Diamond and walked into the kitchen, carrying the empty can. She was a petite woman in her early 50s with a little extra weight, and was vibrant and energetic despite her arthritis. Her hair was jet black, the blackest hair Diamond had ever seen, and she always wore a bright rose red lipstick.

"Abuela, your lipstick is like, so ghetto fabulous!"

"Thanks, dear." Softer: "I think."

"That was a compliment."

"You young people have your own language."

"I bet you did too when you were my age." *If you ever*

remember being my age. That would have been a long, long time ago.

Abuela brought the guava, along with a large chunk of her homemade *tres leches* cake that Diamond loved. The wet, milky cake melted in her mouth as she savored every bite, knowing that her mother would be in meltdown mode if she knew about the massive dose of sugar she was ingesting. But Marsha was far away, busy working in her Manhattan office.

****

The next week at Abuela's was almost overwhelming. Diamond felt isolated from her life and friends. Abuela did her best to be good company, but Diamond felt alone, and being caged up in her grandmother's apartment with its old, quaint furniture and plethora of air fresheners drove her crazy. School work was a distraction, but when she was finished with it, MTV and all the cool CDs sent regularly from Sadie didn't do much to help pass the time. The tutor took up a few hours here and there, but, while helpful, it wasn't quite enough of a distraction. She missed the bustle of school, all the noises of lockers slamming, friends chattering, bells going off. She missed dodging around the press of students going to and from classes, jockeying for a good spot in the lunchroom, trying to find a reasonably quiet corner in the library.

"I am so freaking bored," she said when she was confident her grandmother was out of earshot.

But then Tamara and Shayna paid their first visit since she'd gotten out of the hospital, and it brightened Diamond's world. They talked about everybody and everything until Diamond was exhausted, but she was determined to hang in there, and she tried not to let them see how tired she was.

Tamara said, "What is it about guys?"

"What do you mean?" Diamond asked.

"Guys," she continued. "Why are they so proud of farting?"

Shayna added, "Yeah, I know what you mean! Today, Carlos Harper cut one loose in English class. Loud. When the teacher left the room, it was a symphony of arm farts and burps from his friends chiming in on his stink bomb. They were high fiving until Mrs. Tripp caught wind what was happening and let them have it."

Diamond burst out laughing. "Caught wind?"

"Okay, wrong word choice."

"Let them have it? How?"

"She gave them all a bunch of extra pages to read by tomorrow," Tamara said.

"What about Adam?"

The glance between Tamara and Shayna left no doubt that there was bad news here.

But Diamond persisted. "Come on, don't hold out on me."

"Um . . . Adam and Adora have been making out in the halls a lot lately. She's such a slut," Tamara said.

"I saw them eating each other's faces in the stairwell," Shayna added. "Sorry girl, but you insisted on knowing. But she makes out with other guys, too, when Adam isn't looking. She really is a slut. She'll lock lips with anything." A pause. "Sorry, Diamond, but you asked."

"Yeah, it's okay. I'm cool." The news, though not surprising, debilitated Diamond, and roiling nausea crawled around in her stomach.

When their ride came to pick them up, Diamond zoned out on the couch and listened to "Seasons of Love" from *Rent* on her iPod. One particular hook in the song had extra meaning to her. "…525,600 minutes." It was about measuring the life of a man or woman. 525,600 minutes came out to 8,760 hours, or 365 days. One year.

Did Diamond have a year? She thrust that thought aside, remembering people at the hospital telling her how important it was to keep a positive outlook.

Instead, she focused on the music. She thought it would bring her father back for one of their cerebral imaginary visits that she cherished so much.

"Papa, how will my life be measured? Will it count? Who will remember me?"

There was no answer.

Yeah. Right. Even her imaginary papa wasn't paying attention to her.

Life was sucking right now, the positive attitude thing not working. Adam had fallen into Adora's grip, so all hope was gone there. And she'd probably never see Trey again. Well, hopefully she wouldn't have to see Trey again . . . hopefully she'd never need breathing therapy again. Still, she tried to relive the kiss that she'd replayed over and over in her head, but even her memories of that pleasant moment were fading already.

Although she'd left a message at the hospital for Jessica to call her, three days had passed and still she hadn't heard anything. *She wouldn't call now for sure*, Diamond thought as she wallowed in self pity. *She's too busy. She has other patients.*

The song changed. Diamond continued to listen to her iPod, at the same time watching TV reruns and dozing off and on stretched out on the couch. She woke up an hour or so later, startled after dreaming restlessly about the chemo. The music had ended.

Gross! So wack!

The little pieces of sleep hadn't brought the rest that might help her, and she was still exhausted as she joined her mother and Abuela for dinner. She had no appetite. In fact, the smell of Salma's famous roasted pork with tomatoes, onions, olives, and wine made her nauseous. She picked at her food, but the few bites were so good that she tried to eat a little more. Nobody could cook pork like Abuela!

She noticed that her mother was also picking at her food. Marsha wouldn't look directly at anyone, and she was nervously sitting on the edge of her chair and glancing at the clock every few minutes.

"Mama? You all right?"

No reply. Then a quick, "I'm fine. Just fine. I'm okay."

Great. Back to fine and okay again.

But something was wrong here. Maybe a bad day at work. Diamond prayed it was a bad day at work and not a bad call from some doctor. "Who are you and what have you done with my real mother?" Diamond quipped.

"Diamond's right," Albuela agreed.

"I'm fine. Really, mom." Marsha twirled her fork in the potatoes, the hint of a smile playing at the edge of her mouth.

"Marsha, you're acting like you did when you were a teenager and had a secret boyfriend."

"Boyfriend?" Marsha asked, fumbling to keep the fork from falling. "Boyfriend? Why ever would you suggest something like that?"

"Oh my God," Diamond whispered. In that instant, she tried to imagine her mother as a teenager. Depressing! But not as depressing as the idea of her mother with a boyfriend, holding hands, making out or even worse . . . hitting it! That was so twisted!

"Mama, do you have a—"

"It's work. That's what's on my mind. I've been so busy at work."

Diamond breathed a sigh of relief. So, a bad day at work. Not a bad call from the doctor.

"I met someone at work . . . we had lunch together. It's no big deal. It's only for fun, nothing serious. You know." Marsha blushed.

"Oh my God." This time Diamond said it a little louder than she'd intended.

"It's nothing serious."

"Nothing serious?" Diamond certainly did not know whether or not it was serious. Her mother couldn't go on dates! She was too old. She was thirty! And besides, Marsha belonged to her! What would she do without her mom? What would she do if she had to share her mom? Her mom shouldn't be thinking about men when Diamond had the chemotherapy and pills and lymphoblastic leukemia to deal with. Hello, Mama! L-y-m-p-h-o-b-l-a-s-t-i-c l-e-u-k-e-m-i-a . . . no time to think about boyfriends.

Was that why Marsha had wanted Diamond to come stay with Abuela? The real reason? So she could hook up with some guy from work . . . who was probably only interested in sex because why else would someone be interested in her thirty-year-old mother? Would she take him to the apartment sometime? Had she already taken him to the apartment without telling anyone? Would they do it on the couch? Had they done it on the couch?

"Gross!"

"What did you say, Diamond?"

Oh, God, had she said that out loud?

"I was just saying how great Abuela's cooking is. Nobody can fix pork like her! You're the bomb when it comes to cooking pork, Abuela!"

"The . . . bomb? I swear, I'll never understand your language, Diamond."

Chill, girl. Get a grip.

Her grandmother turned all her attention on Marsha. "I think that's great, a lunch date," Abuela said, eyes fixed on her daughter. "It's about time you met somebody. Way past time. You should indeed go out."

"Oh, yeah . . . it's terrific." Diamond decided she'd never sit on that couch again.

"Honestly, it's nothing serious. We're just friends."

"Well, maybe it's a good idea to make a new friend," counseled Salma. "Is that okay with you, Diamond? That your mother has a new friend?"

"What's wrong with your old friends? They're pretty fresh," Diamond challenged. "But, sure, Mama. I can't wait to meet him. Bring him over soon, okay." God, she didn't mean it. She said it but she didn't mean it. "I bet he's nice." She didn't mean that either.

Marsha changed the subject. "Baby, when's the tutor coming?"

"Tutor? Oh, yeah. Wow. In a few minutes. I better get ready."

Diamond couldn't get out of the kitchen fast enough. In her room, she slumped down on her unmade bed and hugged her teddy bear. She wanted to crawl under the covers and set up a permanent encampment there.

But she couldn't. That lame tutor would soon be here. She wanted to zone out to some music and "talk" to her dad again. But she didn't really want to, because she felt like she'd have to tell him about her mother's boyfriend. And she didn't like to contemplate the notion of her mother having a boyfriend.

She didn't need to compete for her mother's attention and affection right now.

How could you do this to me, Mama? My world's small, I have only a few people, and I've already lost Jessica from the hospital. And you don't even want to live with me. You have me here at Abuela's. You'd rather be with some strange man from work than be with me! And, God, I know I'm being selfish. I know I shouldn't be so selfish. But I just can't help myself right now. I'll apologize to you and Mama later.

Marsha stuck her head in the door for a quick goodbye. In three steps, she was across the small space, leaning over Diamond to give her a reassuring hug and a peck on the cheek. Diamond grunted a reply, but didn't even look up.

She turned up her iPod, but her beloved music couldn't bring her imagined father back into her head. She couldn't get into the tune, and was stuck on the stupid bed being stared at by a vintage Madonna poster . . . left over from when her mother occupied the room years and years and years ago. Arrrgh! This room was even smaller than her room at home. Would her mother take "her friend" from work there tonight? Convenient that Diamond was here at Albuela's. Convenient that her mother had the apartment all to herself.

"I am so not zoning out on our couch ever again," she muttered.

She noticed that her mother had left.

Everybody's abandoning me! There's no one left for me now but Abuela. This is going to be the longest stretch of my so-called life. Hey! At least it can't get worse. I mean, like, what else can happen? What else can possibly go wrong?

****

Later that evening as Diamond in her too-large Hello Kitty pajamas lay in bed, she remembered asking what else bad could happen, almost having to laugh or cry. She had spent two ridiculous, lengthy hours with the Tutor from Hell. That had been bad. Really, really bad.

Mildred O'Murphy's most prominent characteristic was her wicked stinky breath. Mildred was a sixth grade teacher who talked slow; Diamond practically fell asleep between her words. She was trying to teach Diamond history, and droned on about taxes and trade embargos until the young cancer patient was about to wig out.

I'd rather have a root canal without Novocaine, Diamond thought after the first hour. *That couldn't possibly be as painful. Sheesh, I could learn this on my own by reading the book or watching the History Channel. Couldn't the school system have dredged up someone with a little more spark . . . a little more interesting . . . someone who used mouthwash?*

Finally, gratefully, the tutoring session ended and Diamond took the Dr. Pepper and *tres leches* cake Abuela offered, retreating to her room for a safe sugar rush. She grudgingly admitted that a tutor was better than nothing . . . though certainly not better than school. Was the school system paying for this? Did it come out of her mother's good old American tax dollars? Or was her mother paying for the tutor out of her own pocket? One more bill to siphon away whatever savings her mother might have left. Was her mother going into debt over this? That's something Diamond hadn't thought to ask before. And just as quickly decided she wouldn't ask it; she didn't want to know.

Cut her some slack about the boyfriend, she decided. *Grow up and just cut her a little friggin' slack.*

****

These days were much the same as the first week, as she suspected the third week would be, too. Diamond adjusted to the Tutor from Hell Mildred O'Murphy, and she, Tamara, and Shayna laughed and Skyped about the woman's smelly breath.

Some days, though, were so long and boring that Diamond actually looked forward to "Musky Mildred," the nickname her peeps gave the tutor. It was someone to talk to other than Abuela and her mother; someone different to look at and to share a guava with.

Soon, Tamara and Shayna began to get busy with their own lives, and traveling from Coney Island in Brooklyn to the Castle Hill in the Bronx became too long a trip and a real hassle for them. So their visits dropped off. Diamond understood, though she felt like she was being abandoned again.

Even the time they hung out together online and texting trickled off until it became less and less routine. Leukemia girl was getting lonely.

It's hard to know that they're having fun without me. Their Facebook pages hold photos of everyone hanging out and doing stuff. Should I post pictures of myself puking or hanging out with Musky Mildred? Maybe my post should say: "Today was the same as yesterday as it will be tomorrow.". . . stay tuned . . . yawn . . . a real crowd pleaser.

Most every night, Marsha came for dinner. Diamond endured

the talk about her mother's new "friend" Michael. At least she didn't call him something icky . . . like Mikey. Despite Diamond constantly reminding herself that her mother needed a "life," the only thing she really deep-down wanted to hear about Michael was that he was history.

She missed her mother, and would lie in bed and remember the days before the leukemia came out of remission. They spent more time together . . . and her mother would often ask to do things with Diamond when Diamond turned her down in favor of hanging with Tamara and Shayna.

Diamond's music took a more prominent position in her life. It was her crutch and comfort, her best friend and partner-in-crime, her time-waster and salvation. Diamond lived in it more than ever. It made her dreams so vivid they were almost real.

On a night full of thunderstorms, the music rolling loud through her iPod, her father suddenly returned.

"Oh, Papa, I've missed you so much!"

"I'm never far away, corazón. I've always got your back."

"I miss many people these days, Papa. I've been pretty lonely. And I worry about who will miss me when I, you know . . . die. I mean, who'll actually remember me?"

"I'd remember, corazón, and miss you like crazy. But you're not going to die. You're my Diamond girl, and diamonds are forever as the old song goes. You know about Anne Frank? Good. Well, she wrote

that everybody has a piece of good news inside of them. The good news is that you don't know how great you can be! How much you can love! What you can accomplish! And you haven't begun to realize your potential."

"That's so beautiful, Papa. The Diary of Anne Frank was required reading at school. I read it this past summer. I think about her now and then. I didn't enjoy reading it much. Boring in places, hard to get through. And there's some controversy about whether she actually wrote it. But I think she wrote it. Parts of it were good. Sad, but good."

"Then be inspired by her, corazón. Hang in there and wait for good news."

"Oh, I will, Papa! Thank you so much!"

"You'll start feeling better. You'll get to know your real potential."

"And we can go dancing?"

"We're going to dance a lot, corazón, you and me. We'll get in my Porsche and go dancing anywhere you want."

"Papa, do I look like you?"

"Absolutely, dark hair, dark eyes. But you're better looking. Much, much much better looking. You're beautiful, Diamond."

"Oh, Papa. You really have a Porsche? That's awesome! I can't wait to see it. And I can't wait to introduce you to Nuyorican . . ."

Interrupting her fantasy, Abuela was calling her, so Diamond reluctantly released her father and the music, stuffed the iPod in her nightstand drawer, and dragged herself to the kitchen. She realized she hadn't been out of the apartment in a long time, days and days, and the walls were slowly and surely closing in on her. This was a prison, a quaint air-freshener filled prison, and her grandmother was the warden.

"Marsha called earlier, Diamond. She's bringing Michael to dinner tonight. Isn't that a nice surprise? We will finally get to meet him."

Arrrrrrggggghhhhhh. For this news I turned off my music? I'd rather get ten ingrown toenails and a dozen root canals before I'd meet Michael. Surprise. Lovely. Root canals without Novocaine.

"Dinner will have to be just right."

"You're making your special meatloaf?"

"Why yes, it's a special occasion. One I hope will be repeated many times."

"I think I'm gonna barf," Diamond mumbled in a sick voice.

"What, dear?"

"I said I'm going to get ready. I can't let her . . . friend . . . see me in this."

"I almost forgot. Michael is bringing his son. He's about your age, I think."

"What a drag," Diamond muttered.

She fled the kitchen on legs that turned increasingly to jelly with each step. She really was going to throw up by the time she reached her room, which again she reminded herself was no bigger than a closet.

But a trip to the bathroom resulted in nothing but the dry heaves.

Does this mean I'll have a troll as my brother and a weird stepfather? Maybe they're not that bad. No, they're worse. I can't do this! The timing is so wrong! Please, God, don't let Mama be serious about this man. She doesn't need a boyfriend. Well, maybe she needs a boyfriend, or thinks she needs one, but I don't need her to need a boyfriend. I just need her to need me.

Diamond clutched her bear and thought of the fire escape, perhaps climbing down it to run away. Down the block maybe her real dad would pick her up in his Porsche—vroom! A good plan except for the fact she was in her Hello Kitty pajamas, barefoot, and it was pouring down hard sheets of chunky rain that had turned everything not concrete into mud.

Nuyorican Knockout sensed Diamond's pain and, within seconds, she was at her side, zooming there on her swag surfer, hair streaming behind her in the wind. The bleak rain suddenly stopped and the sun began to shine. Not that weather-control was one of Nuyorican's powers, it just seemed to cooperate with her wishes this day.

Birds chirped, and a sweet, warm air blew through Diamond's open window as she was gently lifted by her alter ego super hero big booty friend into the vast, peaceful sky. Nuyorican hadn't yet found a cure for cancer, but she assured Diamond that she was still working on it and wouldn't be dissuaded by all the other superhero tasks she was at the same time confronting. After all, curing Diamond and lots of other young people like her was the top priority. She would get Diamond back into that eighty . . . ninety . . . one hundred percent survival rate.

The city was cleaner up here, so high up Diamond couldn't see the soda cans and candy wrappers, the empty McDonald's bags that littered the sidewalk. She couldn't see the homeless people by the train stop, and she couldn't hear the stray dogs bark and beg for scraps. Neither could she hear the music that pulsed like a heartbeat in the neighborhood, the feel-it-through-the-pavement beat that gave the area its color. But the sky had its own music, birdsong and the whoosh of the air passing by.

Diamond wished she could stay up here for hours. Then she wouldn't have to meet her mother's boyfriend and his geeky son.

Arrrrrrrgh.

****

Abuela had to call Diamond twice, as she was lying in bed trying to decide what to wear. Finally, she got up in a defiant mood. She wasn't going to get dressed. If Hello Kitty was good enough for her bear, it was good enough for Michael and his stupid son. She didn't want to look nice. She wanted to look like this year's Leukemia Poster Child. With luck, that would drive them away.

She dragged herself into the living room, ignoring the disapproving look on Abuela's face. Her mother's back was to her, and she coughed to get Diamond's attention. She said, "Michael, this is my daughter. Diamond . . . this is Michael Harrison."

Marsha was clearly shocked to see Diamond's appearance, but Diamond avoided her mother's eyes and looked at this Michael dude, who happened to be gorgeous.

Not at all what she expected.

Not at all what she wanted to see. She wanted to see some pimply-faced, overweight, balding jerk that her mother would wake up and ditch by next Tuesday. She wanted to see air where Michael was standing. Diamond wanted the man to melt like the Wicked Witch of the West.

His startling eyes reminded her of somebody, but she couldn't place it. Then Michael stepped aside, and his son, Adam Harrison—

her Adam Harrison, Mr. Bad Boy Adam Harrison—stood facing her.

Adam was speechless, staring at her in her overlarge Hello Kitty pajamas.

She was speechless.

And embarrassed.

And wigless.

Diamond's mind raced at warp speed.

This is impossible. How could this be? I don't believe this! Oh—my—God! Put this all on rewind! Let me have gotten dressed! Let me have put on my wig! Let me have looked like . . . something else. What is he doing standing in Abuela's living room, staring at me? I'm toast!

Diamond looked away and moved backward, almost stumbling. She couldn't escape the living room fast enough. Her mind's eye gave her an instant replay of what had occurred: Leukemia Poster Child holding a little bear and wearing Hello Kitty pajamas, with her hair—what little hair she had—looking like a nest for dysfunctional rats.

Marsha followed her into her room, but Diamond didn't give her time to say a word.

"Mama, how could you? *THAT WAS ADAM!* THE Adam! And you brought him here? Without warning me? I can't believe you did this to me!"

"Calm down, baby. What are you talking about?"

"Mama, we're in school together! That's the boy I've been

crushing on all year! Now you brought him to Abuela's crappy little apartment! This is so wack! Look at me! I look horrible, and he'll go to school and talk smack about me with Adora and everybody. I'm never going back to school! Never ever ever ever."

Diamond's tirade caught Marsha off guard. They stood glaring at each other.

Marsha's mouth worked, and Diamond knew she was praying, probably trying to find the right words.

Diamond tried to imagine music in her head, hoping to bring back her fantasized father who would whisk her away in his Porsche. Calling out to Nuyorican Knockout to take her back into the sky.

"Baby, I had no idea! I didn't know Michael's Adam was *your* Adam. I didn't even think about his name. What a small world! What are the chances? I'm stunned and sorry, but right now we have guests in the living room and we have to be polite, so we'll . . . we'll talk about this later."

Diamond was breathing so hard, making a huffing sound like a train.

"Do you want me to ask them to leave? I could tell them you're not feeling well."

Diamond paused and took a deep breath. "Leave? That'd be so . . . lame. They'd know it was because I didn't want them here." *And I don't want them here. I don't want to be here.* "I don't have any appetite, so I'll just give dinner a miss and zone out here in my room." A pause: "Just tell them I don't feel like eating tonight. You and Abuela and Michael and Adam have a good time."

"Come on, just put on some lip gloss and your favorite sweater and come out and spend some time with us."

Diamond defiantly ignored her wishes.

Marsha gave a sad shake of her head. "Alright, baby, if that's what you want to do. Try and relax. I love you . . . are you going to be okay?"

"Yeah. Fine. Okay." *Fine and okay again. Fine and okay.*

"I'm really sorry Diamond. How could I have known?"

"I guess you couldn't have known," Diamond mumbled, thinking to herself, *I totally blew it. There he was, Adam Harrison in Abuela's living room, looking fine. I wanted Mr. Bad Boy to notice me, but not this way! Oh, he noticed me all right. He noticed me to the point that he'll tell everyone at school about leukemia girl in her big Hello Kitty pajamas with what little bit of hair she's managed to keep. Dear, God, take me now!*

Diamond retreated to her bed, bear, and music, trying not to think about what a fool she'd just made of herself. But instead thinking of nothing but that. She wondered what kind of brief, skanky nightgown Adora probably wore. And had Adam seen her in it?

No! No way am I gonna think this way! I'm Diamond Lopez,

the big booty Nuyorican superhero—and I'm gonna prevail! I'm gonna prevail over cancer and living here at Abuela's and I'm gonna somehow forget this horrible, rotten, miserable night ever happened.

Hello Kitty. Dear God, Mr. Bad Boy saw me in Hello Kitty.

Just Friends

The next day, Diamond felt worse than she had any time before, during, or after being in the hospital. The nausea was relentless as she threw up Frosted Flakes after breakfast. She lay in bed, trying to amuse herself by making a joke about wearing Hello Kitty pajamas and feeling as weak as a kitten.

She didn't know what made her sicker, her mother's relationship with Michael or the way she'd made such a goof of herself in front of Adam. She imagined Adam and Adora mocking her while they were sucking face in the stairwell. She tried to hide from Abuela how rotten she felt, and was successful at it, but not so much with her mom after supper that evening.

Diamond started by begging off on any talk about Michael.

Marsha put a hand on her girl's sweaty forehead to check for a fever. She asked a couple of questions, to which Diamond only mumbled answers. But when she had to hurry to the bathroom twice in ten minutes, her brave and self-assured facade crumbled to the ground.

"Oh, baby, come here."

Diamond surrendered to her mother's arms and sniffled out her misery. But when a return to the hospital for tests was mentioned, the leukemia girl pulled away.

"Mama, I'm not that sick at all! It's just a reaction to everything that happened yesterday. Meeting Michael and showing Adam that I'm a total loser was too much for one day. I bet that's why I'm feeling like this."

Marsha listened sympathetically, and they had what Diamond considered "a good girl talk session." Her mother stayed longer than usual, and they were even able to laugh a little, particularly about the "Tutor from Hell," who was now officially called TTFH.

Marsha mentioned the hospital one more time.

Diamond showed some energy. "No. Not now. Not yet."

Marsha drew her lips into a thin line. "We'll see what tomorrow brings."

Tomorrow was a little better, and so talk of the hospital was temporarily shelved.

As the next few days passed, Diamond felt a little better, had

a little more energy, and had reconnected with Shayna and Tamara—
even though phone calls had entirely replaced their in-person visits.
She eagerly waited for her cell to ring every afternoon. But when she
said "Hello" on Friday, she was startled to hear a boy's voice.

"Hi. How you feeling?"

Bummer. Wrong number, though there was something familiar
about the voice.

"Feeling? S'okay, I guess." *Who was it on the other end?*

"Diamond? It's Adam. Got your number from Shayna. Hope
you don't mind me calling."

Say something! Something witty, cool and clever!

"Oh, I don't mind, Adam. Not at all." *Yeah, Diamond, way clever.*

Long, awkward silence. Had he hung up on her?

"Sorry to hear you've been sick. Too bad about the other night,
you not feeling up to dinner or anything. Really miss seeing you at
school every day."

"You have?"

"Well, everybody has, Diamond."

"Oh. Everybody." *Her words should be honored for posterity.*

"I really admire you, Diamond. I mean, the way you've
handled such a long, serious illness. Don't know if I could do it. Well,
actually, I know I couldn't do it."

"Well, uh, thanks, Adam." *God, even his voice was hot!*

And she loved saying "Adam" to him. *Adam. Adam. Adam. What a beautiful word.*

"Diamond, would it be okay if I dropped by there after school one day soon? Just to visit a little."

"Drop by? Oh, sure, Adam. That'd be cool." *You could bring a suitcase, stay a couple of weeks. God, my heart has to be pounding so loud he can hear it.*

"Great, Diamond! How about Monday? I could come by after my last class."

"Yeah, great, Adam. I'd like that." *I'd love that, actually. Monday. Let Saturday and Sunday just disappear. Let it be Monday now.*

They said goodbye, and Diamond sat there without moving, as though bodily motion would break the spell. She saw her bear sitting there and grabbed it, holding it tight to her heart.

"But it *is* real, Bear! He really did call me! "

Big booty Nuyorican super girl danced in front of the mirror for about half a minute until she collapsed on the bed and had trouble catching her breath. Then the phone rang again. She snatched it right up, hoping for some reason it was Adam again, that he had something else to say so she could listen to that delicious voice. But Shayna didn't even give her the chance to say hello.

"Did he call? Were you talking to Mr. Bad Boy? He asked me for your number and told us he'd call you. So . . . did he call?"

Shayna and Tamara took turns on the phone. They seemed as excited as Diamond. They went on and on and on until Diamond was exhausted and having trouble breathing, but no way was she changing this mood.

When they finally hung up, Diamond had to take a long snooze. She woke with a start and sat up in the bed. She'd dreamed she was trapped in that Amsterdam attic with Anne Frank. In the attic, they ate hard bread and cheese from which they picked the mold off. They talked about life, death, remembering, and the future. Anne talked about the unknown, embracing it as part of their lives. *"And we must live our lives to the fullest. Live each day that way."*

Diamond hugged her bear even tighter, closed her eyes, and thought about the Anne Frank dream and about her own life. Living life to the fullest, no matter what misery you're suffering.

"Carpe diem!" her fantasized Papa had said once in a music-dream. *"Seize the day! Grab the moment! Yes, don't merely hang in there, but prevail!"*

"Carpe diem." Some long-dead Roman writer had said that first. She didn't remember who. "Not just endure, but prevail!" Another writer had said that.

Something had given her a new sense of hope and a feeling of peace. Was it Adam's interest in her? Was that all it took to make the world seem okay again?

Okay.

Fine.

Everything was more than okay and fine now.

Throughout the weekend, Diamond tried to fulfill her fantasized father's words of prevailing. But, for most of the time, enduring was all she could manage. Her nausea had miraculously lessened and issues with her mother and grandmother suddenly seemed unimportant, though she still hid from both of them the number of times she still had to hurry to the bathroom.

All day Sunday she looked forward to Monday, and on Monday morning she was up earlier than usual. Her spirits soared as the hours crept along. A long shower finally took her to noon.

Now, what should I wear? My royal blue top? Or maybe the fiery red one with the plunging neckline? Yeah, the plunging neckline will do. It's totally bonita! She applied a touch of make-up.

At two, she was sitting in the living room trying not to watch the clock's crawl toward three. She reasoned four was the earliest Adam could arrive.

Diamond jumped out of her skin when the phone rang. But it was only Tamara. "Any sign of Mr. Bad Boy? I can't wait to hear about it!"

"Not a word, I'll let you know. Now, please get off the phone."

"You go, girl!" Tamara hung up.

Diamond put the phone away and saw that it was ten until four, and a sudden worry struck her: What would she and Adam have to talk about? She was so out of the loop about what was happening at school. She had no idea what Adam liked or didn't like, thought was funny or not funny. Music? Movies? Did he like to dance?

Get a grip, girl! I'm starting to trip! He may not even show up.

Diamond spent the longest afternoon of her life on that sofa, trying not to look at the clock. At half past five her last hope died, and she dragged her sorry self back to the bed. She didn't take calls or texts from Shayna or Tamara. They'd only want to talk about Adam.

Papa, why didn't he come or at least call?

When the doorbell rang, she ignored it. Abuela had ordered pizza and Marsha would be here soon.

No chance it could be Adam, could it?

It was the pizza, and it was a mostly silent dinner, marked by Diamond's realization that her mother did not mention Michael. Did this mean he was toast? This was the first time they'd shared dinner that the word "Michael" wasn't spoken even once. Was this why Adam hadn't come? And wouldn't ever? Had her mother broken up with Michael . . . something she suddenly didn't want to have happened.

Dinner was miserable and, to make matters worse, in a few minutes she'd have to endure two hours of Musky Mildred.

The phone rang in the living room, and at first she thought it might be Adam.

Diamond had retreated to her iPod, telling herself it couldn't be Adam.

And it wasn't. But two minutes later she felt like dancing and singing, because TTFH had called to cancel tonight's session.

"She had some kind of oral surgery," Abuela said.

"A breath transplant, I hope?"

Diamond was on the sofa when the doorbell rang at 7 pm. Bored and expecting nothing, she shuffled to the door in her pajamas (she'd ditched the plunging neckline at 6), and opened it to find Adam standing there. She was annoyed that he hadn't called and that she'd burned through so much nervous energy all day only to have him show up hours late to find her completely unprepared. But then again, he never did specify a time. He'd only said, "after school."

At least Hello Kitty had been washed this morning.

"Hope it's not too late, Diamond. Got tied up after school."

"No, it's fine, Adam. Come on in."

God, why did I change out of that sweater? He's gotta think I'm such a pathetic loser.

"I brought you this. Shayna told me you like *The X-Men* and your favorite character is Storm. This is the latest issue of their comic book. I picked it up yesterday from the newsstand."

"You like Storm, too?"

"She's the bomb!"

They sat on the sofa, drinking guava juice and talking. Diamond found that they liked a lot of the same things, including guava juice. Talking to Adam was so much easier than she expected it to be. Her only difficulty involved not getting lost in his deeply unlimited eyes.

Diamond revealed that she had worn one of her best tops earlier, waiting for his visit, then ditching it a little while ago in favor of comfy pajamas.

Adam revealed that he had once missed a chunk of school from mononucleosis. "Nothing as bad as what you have to deal with, Diamond. But I kind of know what you're going through. Between the mono and us moving, I lost a year of school. So I can sympathize. A little bit, anyway. You're the only person who could do this, go through all of this, and laugh about it. You rock, girl!"

"Why, thank you, Adam."

So very, very easy to get lost in his eyes. She found herself staring at his lips, wondering what kissing him was like.

"When I was sick that time, with mono, the school sent this tutor who was way wack. I mean, she'd drone on and on and her breath was, like, if I got too close, my eyes would start watering."

"Musky Mildred! She was supposed to come tonight but canceled because of oral surgery. Maybe it was a breath transplant."

"I don't remember her name. But I like that . . . Musky Mildred . . . you're too funny, Diamond." Adam laughed out loud as Abuela brought them more guava and two chunks of her famous *tres leches* cake. "Mmmm! This cake is so good! I haven't had anything like it before. It's sweet like you, Diamond."

She turned as red as a pomegranate.

The evening got better and better, but soon it was ten, and Adam said, "Man, it's so late. I gotta go."

At the open door, Diamond and Adam stared into each other's eyes. His lips were slightly parted as he moved closer to her. Oh, God, he was going to kiss her! She remembered Trey's kiss and was glad to have had that experience. Adam's breath was warm on Diamond's face and her lips were parted in anticipation. She closed her eyes and then Adam kissed her . . . on the cheek!

"I'm glad we're becoming friends, Diamond. I really enjoyed tonight. See you later."

"Yeah, Adam, me too. I'm glad we're friends. See you."

Diamond closed the door and moped her way to the sofa. Friends. *Yeah. The boy I've dreamed about, giving me only a little kiss on the cheek to end the night. The only time I've ever really been kissed, I had to beg for it, and that was in the hospital.*

Later that night, as Diamond headed to the bathroom one more time, she attributed her worsening condition to depression, disappointment, too much cake, and too little dinner, rather than a possible worsening of her illness. Sleep was fitful and dreams that she couldn't remember plagued what sleep she did get. But she felt better the next morning, managing to get down half a bowl of Frosted Flakes.

She found the copy of *The X-Men* that Adam had brought her. The graphic novel pulled open Diamond's memories of last night with Mr. Hottie. More likely, Mr. Nottie. She read about Storm, one of her favorite superheroes, but couldn't concentrate. Adam's face swam on every page.

He was drop-dead gorgeous.

He sat right there last night, inches away. It was the best night of her life, until he kissed her on the cheek and declared she was now his "friend." Though disappointed, she had to keep reminding herself that at least he had stopped by. And the time they spent had been fun.

And he did bring her a comic book.

Abuela had gone out shopping and to have *café con leche* with friends. Diamond had never felt so alone. The apartment seemed alien, almost threatening. She couldn't disturb her mother at work, and Shayna and Tamara were in class.

God, there are so few people in my life. Oh, Papa, where are you?

She stood up, checking an impulse to bolt out the door. She'd been trapped in this place for weeks . . . but it felt like months, years, centuries, maybe even millennia.

Once again, Diamond sought the solace of her guava juice, bear, and music. "Song Cry" by Jay-Z played in her ears. It fit her mood. Anne Frank came to mind, enduring all that time in her tiny attic world. She felt ashamed of herself when she thought about Anne Frank's strength and passion.

"I should be inspired by her thoughts of a brighter tomorrow," she said to her bear. "No, I don't know what's going to happen in the future. But neither does anybody else. I have to concentrate on the positive side of the unknown, because it is a real part of my life, and I have to live life to its fullest."

I have to prevail.

Diamond changed to more upbeat music, "Here Comes the Sun" by The Beatles. She sang along with George Harrison.

"One of my favorites, too, corazón."

"Oh, Papa, you always know when to come for a visit!"

"Despite your singing, you seem kind of down. Boyfriend trouble?"

"I wish he was my boyfriend. But last night he kissed me on the cheek, saying he was glad to have a new friend. I'm only his friend! I wanted to be a whole lot more than friends."

"A lot of romances start out as friendships. There's more to a relationship than kissing, corazón. Did he go to any trouble to see you last night?"

"Oh, yeah, Papa, he must have spent, like, three hours all

together on the train."

"Then, maybe there's more than friendship on his mind. Why not think positively and give him the benefit of the doubt?"

"Thanks, Papa, I will. By the way, I've really been trying to, you know, keep a positive attitude and all. Kind of look at the unknown as an adventure."

"That's great, corazón. I'm proud of you. So, you're enjoying The Beatles again. Did I tell you I once sat in on a session with George Harrison?"

"That's awesome, Papa! I didn't know you were, like, a professional musician. What did you play?"

"It was the guitar."

"Oh, Papa, will you play for me some time? Real soon? Were you famous, Papa?"

"No, I was not famous. And I haven't played in awhile. But I'd love to play for you."

The ringing phone abruptly pulled Diamond from her conversation. She realized the music had ended when a train rumbled past on the overhead track, and then her father was gone. Diamond glared at the phone, which was still ringing.

"Hello," she realized too late that she'd snarled into the receiver.

"Hey, girl, are you blowing us off?" Shayna asked. "We're dying to know about last night."

"How do you know he came here last night?"

"Girl, the whole school knows by now. Adam's been telling everybody."

"He has?" Diamond's spirits soared. Mr. and Mrs. Adam Harrison ran through her mind. "What's he been saying?"

"The boy's been wailing about how brave you are and that he way admires how you get on with your life, no matter how much you're suffering. He thinks you're dope. And Adora doesn't look pleased."

He thinks I'm a friend.

Diamond had nothing to say, having to keep herself from hurling the phone across the room and screaming.

"Hey, girl, you still with us?"

"Yeah, sure, where would I go? And what was Adora's reaction to what Adam said? Other than looking unhappy?"

Now, Shayna was quiet for a moment, and then, "She said that you were such a brave, pitiful little loser thing."

"Was Adam with her when she said that? What did he say? Come on, Shayna, be a real bud and tell me."

"Adam didn't get a chance to say anything before the skank's mouth was covering his."

Silence. Then . . . "Yeah, okay. Doesn't really matter. Adam and I are now friends. He sealed the friendship deal with a kiss on the cheek."

"Bummer, girl. Well, hey, listen, Tamara and I are going to try to get up there to see you this week. We've missed you, girl."

"Yeah, me, too. I've missed you buckets and buckets. Got to go now. Nature's calling."

Diamond really wanted to end that dreadful phone call, but she didn't have to work too hard at it thanks to what would become the first of many bathroom trips that day. She was so weak by dinner that she begged off sitting at the table with her mother and grandmother. After dinner, Marsha sat on the edge of her bed.

"Diamond, your condition's deteriorating . . . you've been trying to hide it. And we've got to consider the hospital and more tests. I know you don't want it, but it's the truth and we have to face it."

"Guess truth has its uses but I'm, like, no fanatic about it."

"Sometimes lately, *chica*, I can't tell if you're joking or not."

"Sometimes, Mama, I can't tell either."

"Oh, *chica*. I wish I could do something to make this easier."

"Mama, there's one thing you can do. Tell me what Papa looked like. Please, Mama, I don't know what my own Papa looked like!"

Marsha sighed, looking out the window as a train rumbled past. "He had dark hair and eyes, like you."

"I knew it! Was he handsome?"

Her mother nodded. "All right, that's enough about . . ."

"No, Mama! It's not enough. It's not been enough for a long

time." Diamond got feisty when she wasn't feeling well, and thoughts of her leukemia worsening gave her some courage to stand up to her mother. "I have a right to know! Please! Was he a musician? Did he play the guitar?"

"He was a musician, but not a very successful one. And, yes, he played the guitar. Why ever would you ask that? Now that's enough, Diamond. Really, that's enough. That's all I'm going to say about him."

I knew it! No, Mama, that's not enough. And I'm going to keep after you until you tell me everything. And tell me about Michael, too. You haven't said anything about this so-called boyfriend of yours in quite a few days. Did you dump him? Don't dump him.

"Mama, about the tests and the hospital. For one thing, you have to work in the office now, so that rules out a hospital stay . . . a stay with you being there anyway."

Marsha was shaking her head before Diamond finished talking. "I'll have to work something out again. I'll quit if I have to. I can always get part-time work, and we can move back here with Abuela."

"No, Mama! I won't let you do that!" *There isn't enough room for three people in this apartment. There isn't enough room for two!*

"I'll do it if I have to. Your getting well is the most important thing in the world to me."

"Oh, Mama."

"It'll work out right, baby. Tomorrow, I'm going to call Dr.

Goldberg and tell him how you're feeling. No argument on that point, Diamond. And calling him doesn't necessarily mean you'll have to go back into the hospital."

"Okay, Mama. I'm too tired to argue."

"I love you more than anything in the world, Diamond Lopez."

"I love you, too, Mama." A lingering kiss on the forehead, and her mother walked out of the little room.

Diamond closed her eyes and listened to the noises coming through her window from the street. There were distant traffic and people talking as they walked down the sidewalk and, when she heard an ambulance's siren, she had no trouble picturing herself as its patient.

Way dramatic, girl. I'm not even going back into the hospital. And if I did, it won't be in an ambulance. I'll go in style… flying alongside Nuyorican Knockout. And I won't be there long. Nuyorican is going to cure my cancer.

He's So Into You!

The ambulance trip from Abuela's to the hospital was filled with anxiety, but Diamond was much too sick to remember more than bits and pieces of it. What she recalled most clearly about the day was that Adam was supposed to stop by again after school.

And now he wouldn't. Because she wasn't there.

Or perhaps he would, not knowing she was on her way to the hospital.

Again.

She had to admit that for many days she'd been hiding—and, fairly successfully, she thought—how truly rotten she felt. She just didn't want to return to the hospital with all its needles and nurses and tests and prodding and lousy food and "Diamond this won't hurt" even though it did hurt. It hurt all over.

Twice in her room she'd collapsed onto the floor, but she hadn't told her mother, because nothing was more important than talking to Adam on the phone and waiting for his next visit to the apartment.

Then one day she was sitting on the sofa and suddenly she was on the floor writhing like a coiled snake that had been poked by a stick. She knew that Abuela was there, and there were a few other things that surfaced in her memory. But mostly there was searing pain and a lot of strange people hovering over her . . . the paramedics from the ambulance that her grandmother had summoned.

The ride was fitful and filled with the siren wailing, cars honking, someone yelling to "get out of the way, you moron"—then cursing—it might have been the ambulance driver. The siren stopped and there was the ratcheting sound of a door opening.

She woke to find herself in a hospital bed with a tube in her nose, drips in her arm, someone crying in the distance—a voice she didn't recognize—and those distinct hospital cleanser-and-flower smells accompanied by a video arcade of beeping, buzzing monitors.

Diamond turned her head this way and that to see a row of pink bunnies hopping around the walls.

"Oh, no, not again, please," she mumbled, discovering her mouth was dry as sandpaper. Hell must be filled with rows of pink bunnies, she thought.

No one else was in the room. No mother. No Albuela.

She was alone with the wretched bunnies.

The nurse call button? Too weak to reach it. Fear joined the loneliness. Just how sick was she? Was she dying? No pain, not at the moment, but she was more nauseous than she'd ever been. It felt like her stomach was a car on a Tilt-A-Whirl.

A clickety-click from out in the hall interrupted her misery. She strained to look at the doorway, but outside of the pink bunnies, everything looked blurry.

Concentrate!

Someone was coming down the hall, the clickety-click heralding one of those metal pushcarts.

Her vision cleared slowly, and she picked up the smell of lilacs. It was a familiar fragrance. Not flowers, but cologne or perfume.

"Jessica? Is that you?" She could tell that her words were wobbly.

"Nobody else, Diamond. 'It's so good to see you' hardly seems appropriate. But I am happy to see you. If you have to be here, anyway." Jessica's blond tresses came into view and the scent of lilacs was stronger.

Diamond tried to muster a return smile, wondering if Jessica could sense how fake it was. "Water, please."

Jessica put a straw to Diamond's parched lips. The cool water was wonderful.

"No, please, don't take it away!"

But Jessica put the frosted glass on the bedside table. "You don't want to drink too fast and get sick. My bad, as they say! I'll give you more later. Promise."

Diamond remembered that she was mad at Jessica, but couldn't quite recall the reason why. Mad. Mad. Mad. Why? Oh yeah, something to do with Jessica not returning her phone call a few weeks ago. God, it seemed like months ago! She didn't want to be mad, but she didn't like the feeling of being ignored either. She didn't feel the same happiness and relief at seeing Jessica that she usually felt at the hospital. All she felt was anger. But maybe she wasn't so mad at Jessica as she was mad that she was here.

"Your mother should be back soon, Diamond."

"Why did she go?" *And why ever would she leave me alone in this room when I'm sick?*

"Girl, she's barely left this room since you got here."

"How . . . how long have I been here?"

"Let's see. This is the third day."

"Three days? Are you kidding? Three days? That's not possible. Tell me you're kidding?"

Jessica opened her mouth to say something, but there was a clatter from somewhere out in the hall. Someone had knocked over something metallic and it bounced like a drawer of silverware dropping.

"Three days? Not possible."

Diamond's mind was beginning to clear, and she realized that she really *was* mad at Jessica. The perky blonde smile, the lilac scent… it annoyed her. No… it disgusted her. Jessica's smile was so shallow and phony! Why hadn't she noticed this before? Jessica had been nice to her because it was her job, because like all the other nurses she was paid to be pleasant to the people stuck in this place. God, she wanted to get out of here. Get out of here now!

"Yes, three days. Something wrong, Diamond?"

Before she could censor herself, Diamond blurted out, "Obviously something's wrong! What you did was too wack!"

Jessica looked stunned. "I'm sorry Diamond, but I don't know what you're talking about."

"I left you a phone message. You didn't call me back. I needed to talk to you, and you wouldn't call me back. Not even for a few minutes."

There were little metallic sounds now . . . someone picking up the mess.

"You couldn't be bothered, Jessica."

Diamond knew she was acting like a four-year-old having a temper tantrum, but it was too late to take it all back now. She'd started this tirade and now she had to finish it.

"I thought you were my friend. A friend would have called back."

Jessica looked confused at first, then hurt. "I was out of town for a while, girl, visiting family up north. I guess I just didn't get the message. I'm so sorry! I would have called you, Diamond. I *am* your friend."

Diamond really felt lame now. Super-embarrassed. Her mood softened immediately.

"Oh, Jessica, I'm the one who's sorry. I shouldn't have dumped on you like that. It seems I've been dumping on everyone. I have so many people I need to say 'I'm sorry' to."

Jessica leaned over and kissed Diamond on the forehead, and still her face was sad. "Hey, girl, no problem. I knew that wasn't the real Diamond talking . . ."

Someone walking toward the bed cut off Jessica's words.

"Mama!" The word came out a croak.

"Oh, baby girl! You're awake. How are you feeling?"

They hugged and, over her mother's shoulder, Diamond saw such a look of hurt on Jessica's face. Her words had stung the young woman hard, despite her saying "no problem."

"I'll let you two visit," Jessica sighed. Her voice sounded dead.

The child care specialist walked out, and Diamond and her mother got caught up.

Well, admittedly there wasn't much catching up to do. Marsha explained that Diamond had collapsed and passed out. Abuela had called 911, and Diamond was rushed to the hospital.

Diamond noticed that her mother was in nice pants and was

wearing a blue blazer, the shirt under it sporting a faint coffee stain. Marsha had been at work when this happened, and either hadn't changed clothes in those three days or was guzzling coffee and wearing part of it.

"But why did I pass out? Is my illness that much worse? Please tell me the truth, Mama. Don't you sugar-coat anything."

Her mother nodded. "I don't know, and that's the truth. They're doing tons of tests, but they don't know anything conclusive yet. They've got more tests to do over the next few days, they say."

"Let the fun and games begin."

"I won't sugar-coat anything. When they tell me something, I'll tell it straight to you."

"Promise?"

Marsha swallowed hard. "Promise."

"Tests. I'd rather take more tests at school. Math and science and everything else." *God, was that a lame attempt at something funny?* "Did Abuela come to the hospital with me?"

"Of course, Niña. She was here until a little while ago. Her arthritis was acting up from sitting so long at your bedside, so I told her to go home to rest."

"Have I had any phone calls? Or visitors?" *Not that I could've visited with anyone. Out three days. The world passing me by for three days. Was death like this? Days of nothing. Oblivion? Except for more than three days. For eternity. An absolute eternity of nothingness.*

"Tamara and Shayna called a couple times, and there was Adam. He called and said he wanted to come, but for now only family members are allowed to visit."

Adam had called! That was the best possible news. Well, other than a sudden and complete recovery.

"I'm not seeing his father anymore. Not right now. Too much going on here, and with work. Both of us busy. Sometime in the future, maybe. I'm not entirely closing the door on it. But for the time being, it's just me and you."

Diamond felt worse. As much as she'd wanted her mother all to herself, she realized her mother needed . . . something . . . maybe Michael. At least the door wasn't "entirely closed."

She spent the rest of the day dozing, talking to her mother, getting interrupted by nurses and lab technicians who said "this won't hurt" even though it did hurt, but not as much as she'd expected it to, eating some lunch, and listening to her iPod.

Jessica didn't come back.

Diamond was listening to Beyoncé singing about being lonely when suddenly she heard her Papa say, *"You feeling better, corazón?"*

"A little, Papa. Actually a lot, now that you're here."

"Don't forget, I've always got your back."

"I know, Papa. Looks like we'll have to put off our dancing."

"When you're well, corazón, we'll dance and dance and dance to make up for lost time."

"Papa, you make it sound like it's gonna happen. Totes."

"Oh, it is. You'll be a dancing fool. I can't wait to see you on the dance floor at our cool spot. Sparkling like the diamond that you are. Diamonds are the hardest, toughest thing there is. Cut glass like nothing else. You're tough, Diamond."

"I feel more like zircon than diamond, Papa."

"Diamonds are forever, the saying goes."

"I feel like I'll shatter any moment."

"Not for too much longer, corazón. You will feel better. Remember, diamonds are forever! Not only do they endure, but . . ."

"They prevail, Papa. I know."

"Now, get some sleep. Before you get well, there'll be a lot more testing, poking and prodding you. I'll be back soon."

"Papa, don't go!"

But Diamond didn't have a chance to say the words out loud before her eyes closed and she drifted off to sleep.

She couldn't remember any of her dreams.

****

Days passed by, maybe a week or more, time being irrelevant in Diamond's bunny-decorated world. The tests proved to be endless, and no one would ever tell her the results. She was frustrated, growing angry, but also too sick and too weak to put much verbal strength into her rants.

Her mother had promised she'd level with her.

Either her mother really didn't know, or she was breaking that promise right, left, and every which way.

Diamond hadn't asked anyone how long she'd been here. Maybe two weeks? She didn't want to know. Not really. The thought of a lengthy hospital stay was more depressing than any words she could summon up to describe it. And at the back of her mind she worried about the bills. Sure, her mother had insurance through work. But Diamond knew insurance wasn't a "stay in the hospital for free" card.

Two weeks?

Three? *Dear, God, please don't let it be three.*

Diamond began to gain back some of her strength. She knew she had been severely dehydrated and undernourished from not eating much at Abuela's . . . and from puking up most of what she had been shoveling in, so the IV fluids and nutrition in the hospital made a big difference. She was even able to visit the teen room with her mother.

But feeling better physically did nothing to relieve her fear and frustration about not being told the test results.

"You promised, Mama."

"Baby, the results are still pretty much inconclusive. A

few more tests, I promise, and the doctors and I will have enough information to make decisions."

"I'm left out of the process entirely?"

"And to tell you what's going on."

"I lie in that wack bed day after day, and can't have even one visitor? Family only. That's so lame, Mama! And I don't get a word to say about any of it? About what they're doing to me? About what they're testing me for? If I was older, I'd have a say. A few years older and I could tell them no."

"Baby girl, I'm sorry . . ."

"You promised."

"Listen, baby girl . . ."

"Stop calling me 'baby girl!' I'm not a baby! And where's Jessica? Has she deserted me again?"

"Jessica didn't desert you. There was an emergency in her family and she had to rush off to deal with it. She's taken some time off work. I know how sick you are Diamond, but—"

"Do you? Do you know how sick I am? You're not telling me, even though you promised. And now Jessica's gone."

"Jessica . . . other people . . . have serious problems too."

The big booty leukemia patient looked closely at her mother's face, seeing weary, redlined eyes, thinking that her mother had aged visibly in the passing of a handful of days. *Dear God, please let all of this have been only a handful of days.*

"Oh, Mama, I'm sorry for being selfish, especially about you. And I have been so terribly, terribly selfish. Like I'm an alien, not the real Diamond." But it was the real Diamond, she realized. She had become more selfish the sicker she got. "You look exhausted. God, it's been hard on you. What about your job?" *And what about bills? And insurance? And Michael? You should still be seeing Michael.*

"I'm all right, Diamond. I'm fine. Okay."

Fine. Okay. Which meant things were neither.

"I had some vacation time coming, and some sick days, and now they're letting me work at home again. Well, here, actually."

"No, Mama, you're not all right. I'm worried about you."

"Well, when Abuela's arthritis is better and she can stay over here, I promise I'll go home more often. I think the tests are about finished. They have to be."

"Yeah, I can't imagine them needing any more blood. I've given them enough to feed an army of vampires. Maybe that's why I've been feeling so . . . yuck. I don't have enough blood to satisfy them."

Marsha laughed.

Diamond considered it a beautiful sound, like crystal wind chimes teased by a breeze. She hadn't heard her mother laugh for quite a while.

The next day, Diamond opened her eyes from a short snooze

too see Jessica standing by the bed.

"Hi, Diamond, they tell me you're feeling much better lately. Sorry I had to rush off without telling you anything."

"It's cool, Jessica. What about your emergency? Was someone sick or something? In your family?"

Jessica frowned. The wrinkles on her forehead marred what Diamond considered an otherwise perfect complexion. "My aunt. Practically raised me. She had a little setback with her heart, but she's fine now. Thank you for asking."

Diamond realized there was something different about Jessica. "Your perfume, Jessica. The lilac scent. What happened to it?"

Jessica bobbed her head to the side. "Lilac. Well, I used it to cover the hospital smells. You know, all the cleaners they use, and disinfectants. I'm still wearing it. But I was afraid it might be a little too strong for you, so I've been putting on much less."

"Oh, I love that lilac scent. Best smell in the hospital. Well, I guess it's not like being complimented for the best smell in a flower shop." Diamond sucked in a breath. Flowers. She noticed there weren't any flowers in her room. Not from her mother or Abuela or her cousins, who hadn't been in to talk about dancing and Broadway shows and too-cool shoes.

No flowers.

Didn't they care? Or maybe she'd just been in here so much that she'd drained their spending money on all of the previous bouquets.

"I miss smelling the lilacs," Diamond said.

The Jessica smile returned in all its glory. "Thanks. And it's good to hear that the real Diamond is back."

"Well, maybe a little back. If these tests would just end! And if they'd only tell me about the results. My mother said she'd tell me. But all I get out of her is that they're not done yet. I know they're telling her something."

Jessica's smile took on a sad cast. "They're just trying to determine what caused so much weakness in you, and what those nasty cells are up to. You want them to find out, don't you? This is an excellent hospital, Diamond. They can't fix the problem if they don't know exactly what the problem is. But I'm betting that by the middle of next week they'll know something for certain and can make some decisions about whether or not you'll need more chemo. But for now, the doctor says you can start having visitors!"

Adam! We'll be together again! Way soon!

"When?"

And probably flowers. I bet that's why there are no flowers in my room. No visitors other than Mama and Albuela equals no flowers.

"Any time during regular visiting hours. Your mother's already talked to your friends. She'll tell you about it when she comes in."

"This calls for a celebration! Maybe an extra purple blue bunny ice cream in the teen room today."

"Maybe even two extra!"

"Thank you so much for everything, Jessica. I don't know what I'd do without you. And listen, what I said to you before—that was out of line. I really am sorry."

"I know it wasn't the real Diamond talking." Jessica sat on the edge of the bed. "Not to worry. Besides, it's already forgotten. Now, we've got some pigging out to do in the teen room. And there's a brand new video game—first dibs on player one!"

Diamond was grinning broadly as they made their way to the teen room.

****

Shayna and Tamara were the first visitors—and they brought flowers, a bouquet of carnations and daisies that had a helium balloon floating above it with the obligatory "get well" scripted in pink. They all hugged and started talking at once.

"This is great. So like old times," Diamond gushed.

They dished for a couple of minutes, but Diamond only wanted to hear about Adam.

"He's real wired about seeing you, girlfriend. He said to tell you that he's gonna try to come by tomorrow after school. He's so into you, girl!" Shayna tittered.

"Yeah? We haven't even really kissed! Not one time! Well, on the cheek, so that doesn't really count. I'm afraid he's into me only as a friend. And nothing else."

"Yeah, maybe," Tamara said. "But are you ever, like, alone with him?"

"Boy's kind of shy. You got to remember that," Shayna added.

"He's not shy with Adora! Even with lots of people around . . . or so you say."

"Diamond, Adora always makes the first move. Skank's got the fastest lips in school." This from Tamara.

"Yeah, and they're not making out in the stairwell anymore. We haven't seen 'em sucking face anyway. Well, she sucks face . . . but not his. He was probably tired of swapping spit with the skank. Word is he spotted her with other guys, finally realizes she's a slut."

"You know, he might think friends are all you want to be," Tamara said. "Maybe you should, like, kiss him first."

"Listen to what your girlfriend's saying. Make that first move."

"What you got to lose, Diamond? At least, you get to lock lips."

After ten more minutes of talk, the nurse came in. Visiting had to end for the time being, and Diamond was both happy and sad to see her friends go. Sad because she'd missed them terribly. But happy because even their brief visit had exhausted her. Yeah, she had to admit that Jessica was right. The Doctors should test and test and test to find out just why she got so tired so easily. Besides, Diamond was glad to have some time to herself so she could just kick back and think about Adam's visit tomorrow. The suggestion that she take the lead and kiss him kept buzzing in her brain.

But by early evening there were so many other things buzzing around in Diamond's head that she couldn't focus her thoughts of Adam. She thought about Jessica, and how happy she was that they were buds again. She knew things about Jessica now, things that made her seem like more than a perky dumb blonde, like that she had an aunt who'd practically raised her and that she dropped everything to go see her. And she thought about Mama, who was working so hard and whose pretty face was beginning to show the price of all this stress. Her mother looked years older.

And she thought about the other patients in the hospital, the ones roughly her age who she'd seen in the teen room, the younger ones who reminded her of herself when she had the first bout with leukemia, and the older people in other wings. This afternoon she'd overheard two nurses out in the hall talking about a Baptist minister who was getting treatment for a brain tumor at a nearby hospital and who stopped by here to visit children on this floor on the way to his next radiation dose. The minister said it was "God's will" that he had to face cancer and that he hoped to be strong enough to handle the challenge. He said that in one moment of weakness he'd asked "why me?"

Diamond admitted that she hadn't been all that strong and that she'd felt sorry for herself and had over and over and over asked "why me?" She wished she could be stronger for her mother and could face this with courage and determination rather than with a million butterflies flapping away in her stomach and with the selfishness that she'd been exhibiting. All those thoughts buzzed.

The loudest buzzing, though was about the tests they'd been taking for . . . how many days? Or had it been weeks? And the final results. What would they show? What would be done to her? Would she live or die?

Live or die?

No way to think, girl! Remember Anne Frank. Anne had to embrace the unknown—own it body and soul. And she'd had to accept that the unknown could bring positive things, wonderful things.

Carpe diem, girl!

Seize the day!

With both hands, she would. And appreciate that she had this day. Live each day to the fullest, 'cause you never know when it will be your last. Be glad you have it, she told herself. Stop wallowing in pity.

Tomorrow, Adam would be here. It would be Friday. Could she really kiss him first? She remembered Trey's kiss. That was awesome! And Trey said she had kissed really well, hadn't he? Or was she just thinking that he had? But Trey knew the kiss was coming. He was ready for it. How would Adam react?

Why was she making such a big deal about a kiss? Why should she even worry about it? Why should she think about it?

She hadn't seen Trey since that kiss . . . now that she thought about it. A nurse said that he was working on a different floor. Was it because of her? Was he working elsewhere to avoid her? He had mentioned the possibility of losing his job.

Chill, girl. Trey's the past. Adam's the future.

Or maybe she'd die and there would be no future.

Diamond tried to escape into Jay-Z's song, "Can't Knock The Hustle." Finally, she was far from the hospital, and a little later in deep sleep that brought dreams about being in the attic with Anne Frank.

How strange…someone was banging loudly.

Diamond woke up before she knew who was at the attic door. How could Anne Frank know what might come at any moment, yet stay so calm and write about embracing the unknown future and living each moment to its fullest?

Surely, you can do that, girl. You don't have to live knowing that, at any moment, that knock on the door might come.

She realized with a start that it was Friday morning and that she had slept the whole night away and that Adam was coming this afternoon. Breakfast, procedures, getting cleaned up, each little thing seemed to take forever.

Yet it was only ten minutes past ten.

Jessica arrived to save the rest of the morning with her smile and a selection of cute, cheap little open-ended golden rings.

"These are for any place on your body, girl."

"Anywhere? My mother'd wig out at most places I could put a ring. Well, at any place I could put a ring. What do you suggest, Jessica? My belly button? My tongue? My left eyebrow?" Then a sad thought crossed her mind . . . you couldn't really see her eyebrows, the hair having fallen out from the chemo. She just had these little ridges, like a baby Klingon.

Jessica's smile became a look of sly complicity. "You know, officially, I can't suggest that you do anything that freaks out your mother, but . . ."

"These are, like, rings that come right off?"

"Well, what if they're not? You still game, girl?"

"Jessica, you know I'm game for anything. But, I mean, this is way serious. And I—"

"Looks like I got you, Diamond! I'm pulling your chain. They come right off. But your mother won't know this."

"Let's do it! Let's pull her ch—"

A high-pitched wail followed by sobbing cut her off. It had to have come from only a few doors away. "I don't want to!" a girl shrieked. "No more needles!" Diamond couldn't tell the age of the patient. More wailing followed, but it was muted when Jessica closed the door.

"Now, what part of your anatomy do you want to decorate with a ring? Navel? Lip? Tongue? Nose? Both eyebrows?"

"Maybe my nose, Jessica. Don't want to give Mama a heart attack and a stroke."

"One nose ring coming right up."

Diamond picked out a ring and waited while Jessica attached it to her nose. It pinched a bit, but it was tolerable, and it would work for a few minutes.

Jessica pulled out a small mirror. Diamond smiled as she stared at her be-ringed nose. She appeared to be pretty awesome. Maybe she'd leave it in for Adam's visit.

"You look great, girl!"

"And let's do the left eyebrow, too."

"Coming right up."

"Jessica, do you think that something like a nose ring appeals to a boy? I mean, will it impress the dude I'm interested in?"

"I guess that depends on the dude. Is he the one coming to see you this afternoon? Your mother told me. And you're wired today. I can tell that by looking at you. And I can feel the electricity all around you."

"His name's Adam. Wait 'til you see him. He's drop-dead gorgeous! But there's lots more to him than looks."

"Oh yeah?"

"Yeah. He has swagger and sensitivity! And he's smart and likes comic books."

"I can't wait to meet him, Diamond. Hope he doesn't come after I've gone home for the day." Jessica held out a mirror so Diamond could see the rings.

"Jessica, are you married? Do you have children? What do you like to do when you're off work? Sorry. It's totally none of my business."

"Woah, one question at a time. And, no problem, Diamond. No husband, no children. I like to eat out. Chinese. Indian. Love music. Love to dance."

"I love music and I love to dance! Who do you like?"

They talked about music as they hustled over to the teen room, pigging out on purple Blue Bunny bars. Jessica was something else. That girl could really put the chow down, Diamond thought.

It was half past twelve when Jessica left Diamond. After the Blue Bunny feast, the thought of lunch nearly made her barf. Her mother came, and they visited a few minutes before Diamond remembered the nose ring and the eyebrow ring. She'd taken them off because they pinched. Oh well, she'd save them for later and yank her mother's proverbial chain then.

When Marsha left, the love-struck girl started thinking about Adam again and wondering what she would wear when he came to visit. She knew for certain that it wouldn't be the Hello Kitty pajamas. It wasn't like she had a great variety of wardrobe choices. It's hard to dress up a hospital gown, even with its sexy, peek-a-boo booty slit. Oh well, she'd have to concentrate on hair and makeup . . . err, wig and makeup. And whether or not to wear the nose ring.

In the end, Diamond decided to forget the nose ring because she recalled that Adora had a nose ring. *And* a navel ring. And she probably had rings in places Diamond didn't want to think about.

Diamond was propped up in bed, rehearsing how she might kiss Adam, when she caught him standing in the door and staring at her. Looking into those hazel eyes as Adam approached stripped away what little confidence Diamond had about aggressing on him with a kiss.

"You look like you're feeling better, Diamond. In fact, you're looking way good, girl."

He leaned over and gave her a gentle kiss on the forehead.

"Thank you, Adam. So do you. Look good . . . I mean, way good. You know what I mean." *What did I mean? I'm babbling. God, if I tried to kiss him, I'd probably drool on the boy. At least he kissed my forehead. I can still feel his lips there.*

"You look good in that white hospital gown, Diamond. White suits you. Shows off your complexion."

"Ha, ha, ha. We're kind of color coordinated." Adam had on a white shirt, the collar of which looked like it had been pressed.

"Yeah, kind of like we're brother and sister."

God, no, not that! Not brother and sister! I need him to be a lip-locking boyfriend!

"So, how are things at school, Adam?"

Lame, Diamond!

A nurse came in to take Diamond's blood pressure, and the visit got even more lame when the nurse said, "Oh, how nice, Diamond, your boyfriend finally came to see you."

Did leukemia victims get dispensation for strangling wack nurses?

In a flash, the hospital walls began to shake, and the electronics started to spark and sputter. Nuyorican Knockout stood defiantly between the nurse and the young couple, winding up those massive hips for a home run hit that would send the nurse past Jupiter. Before the lame little nurse knew what was happening, she was bounced right out the hospital window on her way to tour the solar system.

The nurse walked out.

Silence.

Lingering silence. Then they both started talking at the same time. Stopping abruptly. More silence.

"School's about the same. Math, too. I seem to have jumped the shark after addition and subtraction."

"Yeah, I was having trouble with math when I had the tutor. The numbers are just a jumble sometimes. Math is getting to be redonkulous."

"Totes."

They had been talking comfortably for ten minutes before Diamond realized how relaxed she was in his presence.

Soon he got up from the bedside chair and sat down on the bed next to her. They were sitting close . . . almost lip-lockingly close. They continued to dish about people at school and, even though Adora's name didn't come up, Diamond wished Adam would dish on that skank. She wanted him to say that he and Adora were history. Their hands were touching on the bed and she could barely concentrate on what he was saying. She didn't really care what he was saying? She was too worried about what to do next.

A minute later, Adam took her hand. Those hazel eyes had absolutely no bottom, and the boy smelled so fine. The lips. Were they closer? *Kiss him! Now!*

And kiss him she did. Or tried to. Because he was trying to kiss her at the same time, and their mouths missed each other at first. It was embarrassing, but only for a second, because they finally kissed . . . a long, lingering kiss that ended much too soon and left them awkwardly laughing in a rush of nervous talk. The moment ended abruptly when a nurse called through the door.

"Sorry, kids, but visiting hours are over."

Get out of here, nurse! Go away! I thought Nuyorican

Knockout sent you out to Pluto.

Diamond didn't express her rage at the nurse, because she

thought she'd get in trouble for it, so the leukemia girl said nothing.

Just stared into Adam's eyes and inhaled the scent of his shampoo.

He leaned over and gave her a quick kiss on the cheek and said,

"This was cool, Diamond. I'll see you again soon."

And then he was gone.

****

Diamond lolled around in bed after Adam left, reliving the

kiss again and again. That kiss! She couldn't wait to tell Shayna and

Tamara. Maybe she wouldn't tell them. Maybe she'd just keep it

between her and Adam. If she told Shayna and Tamara, it might be all

over school. It should be a private thing.

Maybe.

How could she not tell SOMEONE?

The kiss was so vivid, but exhaustion pulled her eyes shut

and she drifted off to sleep. It was a fitful sleep, and when she woke

up, she was startled to find her mother sitting nearby. And she wasn't

alone. Arranged around the room were Jessica, Dr. Goldberg, and a doctor Diamond had not before seen.

So she'd slept away the rest of the afternoon and the evening, and it was the following morning. She could tell by the light that came in through the window. Why? Why? Why was she always so tired?

Diamond looked up into her mother's weary face and saw that she was trying to smile, though without much success. "There's news, *chica*. The waiting's finally over."

"Show time!" Diamond's attempt at levity did nothing to improve her spirits.

She was introduced to Dr. Osborne, a stocky man with salt-and-pepper hair who announced that he was a specialist in bone marrow transplants. Diamond didn't know about bone marrow, but the word "transplant" definitely got her attention, and not in any sort of a good way. Dr. Osborne said that the marrow in bones produced red blood cells and that a leukemia patient has a deficiency of red blood cells.

"That's why you're so tired all the time, Diamond. You need more red blood cells."

"So . . . give me some." She'd said the first thing that popped into her brain. "Like a transfusion."

"That's sort of what we intend. But it's a little more complicated than a simple transfusion. We'd like to do a bone marrow transplant, Diamond," he said. "New marrow will produce the red blood cells that you need. This kind of surgery has been successfully performed thousands of times—"

"But . . ." Diamond knew there was a but.

"But the process is long and involved."

"A transplant? I'm so not ready for this news. And I was so enjoying the tests," she quipped, hoping this whole idea would blow over quickly. "In fact, I was enjoying them so much I thought I should have a batch more."

"I know it's a lot of information to be digested at one time," Dr. Goldberg added, "So I'm leaving these booklets here for you and your mom to read. They'll familiarize you with the process and take some of the mystery out of it. But for now, you need to get some rest."

"Rest? I think that's all I've been doing."

"Some more rest, then. I'll drop by again later to answer any questions you have after reading the booklets."

"And I have a plane to catch," Dr. Osborne said. "It was nice to meet you, Diamond. Don't worry. You're in good hands."

Jessica and the two doctors walked out after giving Diamond and Marsha a pile of reading material to educate them about bone marrow transplants. In the vast silence that followed, a shaken Diamond clutched her mother's hand.

"Mama, this is so weird. I mean… a transplant? Put something from someone else's body into me? Like a sci-fi movie?"

Her mother squeezed her hand. "Calm down, baby. Take a

deep breath. That's right. Let's read through some of these booklets and learn about the procedure. Maybe it won't seem so weird if we understand it better."

Diamond took several breaths but was too weary to read, so she laid there holding and squeezing her mother's hand. She was still holding it when she fell asleep, dreaming that she was in a wack sci-fi movie where a mad scientist was using a shovel to transplant this gross, runny, egg-white-colored wiggling bone marrow into her body.

Pigs and Bunnies

The weekend crawled, filled with dreary, rainy hours.
Diamond's mother kept busy working on a tight deadline, Abuela
visited twice, and Jessica wasn't at the hospital on either Saturday or
Sunday. Diamond guessed she might have been with her aunt.

So Diamond buried herself in music. Roc-A-Fella records and
The Young Money crew became her family, with the company of her
R&B friends Prince, Alicia Keys, and Mary J. Blige.

For longer and longer periods, she closed her eyes, zoned out,
and escaped into her own world.

Nuyorican Knockout appeared at the window,
decked out in flashing pink on her swag surfer. She
hovered there, waiting for Diamond to climb aboard, but

the young cancer patient couldn't get the window open.

Nuyorican stared at her sadly, and Diamond expected her to waggle her fingers and make the glass disappear so she could escape her disinfectant-tinged prison and rocket high above the city.

But the booty-blasting superhero only continued to stare, sparkling eyes fixed on something several yards past Diamond, maybe miles and miles away. She turned up the volume on her own music, an out-of-this world tune with synthesizers and drums and no words Diamond recognized.

When Diamond gave up on the window and stepped back from it, Nuyorican took off, zooming out of sight in the blink of an eye . . . maybe en route to get Diamond more literature on bone marrow transplants.

Finally it was Monday, but it was still raining. It was half past ten when Jessica walked in, and at that moment the sun broke through the clouds.

"I'm so glad to see you, Jessica! You don't know how much I'm glad! I need to talk . . . to somebody . . . to somebody who isn't my mom. She's getting more coffee."

"Good to see you, too, Diamond." She sat on the edge of the

bed. "Now what is it you want to talk about?"

Diamond sucked in her lower lip and tried to find the words. A glance at the pamphlets on the bed stand sufficed.

"A bone-marrow transplant?"

Diamond nodded. "The doctors, two of them, were in here a few days ago and—"

"They know more about those sorts of procedures than I do, Diamond. If it's something medical—"

Diamond touched her thumbs together and took a deep breath. "Yeah, it's medical and not medical. And it's optional, but not optional. Right?"

Jessica looked toward the hall.

"I mean, it's the end of the line, isn't it? The last-ditch effort at fixing me?"

Jessica's face took on a stoic cast. "You're asking me a very hard question, Diamond. I think maybe you should talk to one of those doctors again."

"Oh, I'm sure I will be. But I want to talk to you." Diamond fixed her with one of those tell-it-to-me-straight-I'm-tired-of-sugar-coating gazes.

"I don't know. I can't say. But I do know that if they're recommending it, they think it's the best option. Our hospital has had quite a bit of success with such procedures. You should dwell on that part . . . the successes." She paused. "Feeling well . . . not having to be here . . . dwell on that."

"I read all the pamphlets, you know."

Jessica drew her lips into a thin line.

"Even if I have the transplant, there's a chance it won't help. Or, worse, there's a chance it won't . . . get along with the rest of me, and my body will fight it."

"Graft versus host," Jessica said numbly.

"Graft versus host *disease*," Diamond said. "It can be as bad or worse than the leukemia. So while new bone marrow is supposed to produce red blood cells and boost your immune system, at the same time you can be . . ."

"Allergic," Jessica supplied.

"Yeah, allergic to the marrow. All sorts of bad things can happen. And maybe lots of medicines for the rest of my life. And lots of medicines come with side-effects."

"Diamond, stop thinking the worst." Jessica squeezed her hand. "There are things doctors will give you to keep you from rejecting the bone marrow. There's a lot of research being done on it now. And, like I said, this hospital is known for its successes."

Diamond brightened, but only a little. "Thanks for talking about it."

"I didn't have much to say. Not really."

"But it was enough." *For now.*

"To change the subject . . . tell me about that hazel-eyed boy who visited you Friday. He's real eye candy. I've been wanting to ask about him."

Diamond hardly needed to be encouraged. She left nothing out, including the kiss. And her almost fatal attack of nervousness.

"Wow, girl! Sounds hot! I saw him in the hall before he came in. He was turning heads. When's he coming back? Maybe you could introduce me."

Diamond's enthusiasm evaporated. "I don't know. He didn't say."

"Sweetheart, if he came here once, he'll be back."

"I know that when we get closer to the transplant, I won't be able to have any visitors outside of my family. I read that." She nodded at the pamphlets. "That's so wack, Jessica!"

"That's because they'll be suppressing your immune system and you'll be susceptible to all kinds of germs. You definitely can't be kissing some dude when you're in that condition! For now, you just need to rest as much as possible and not worry."

Diamond slumped back on the bed. Faintly, she heard sirens. Someone coming to the hospital in an ambulance . . . it didn't have the sound of a fire truck or a police siren, which also often could be heard when she listened for them.

"Don't worry. You mean like not worry about Adam making

out with the school skank? Yeah, cut me off from him entirely and watch me relax!"

Jessica snickered, covering her mouth with her hand.

"Diamond, it's been a long time since your doctors were teenagers. They don't think about stuff like that and—"

"A long time? Yeah, like when dinosaurs roamed the earth. How long am I gonna have to wait for this transplant?"

"Back to the medical questions. I told you I can't—"

Diamond steamed ahead, again fixing her with that stare. "What does it involve, the transplant? The pamphlets don't really say. And how long will it take me to recover? They don't mention that either. And the doctors, they didn't tell me. My mom hasn't talked much about it. They won't tell me anything, Jessica!"

"The doctors should be around in a day or two. They want you to read those information pamphlets thoroughly so you'll be prepared with questions to ask them."

"Oh, I've got plenty of questions. Like the ones I've asked you for starters. And—"

"And they'll be by in a day or two—"

"It's already been a day or two! Or three! Longest, dreariest weekend of my life! Jessica, please tell me what's going to happen and how long it'll take!"

There was another siren, but it faded, and an uncomfortable

silence settled between Diamond and Jessica.

Finally, Jessica broke it. "Diamond, it depends on a lot of different things, like how long it will take to find an ideal donor because the cells have to be a perfect match with your own. Your doctors are the best ones around, I promise you that. They do transplants all the time with great success. Remember, I said focus on the 'success.' The main issue is the wait, because we have to find the best possible match between your bone marrow and the donor's bone marrow."

"Is my bone marrow that hard to match? It sounds so icky! They're gonna be putting somebody's bone marrow in my body. Gross!"

"A close relative would be the best match. But your mother and grandmother have been tested, and they don't match."

Diamond's eyes narrowed. Her mother hadn't told her that she and Abuela had been tested. Her mother really hadn't told her anything.

"How about my father?"

"Your father? Well, your mother said he wasn't available. Maybe you should talk to her about it. I'm sure she has her reasons for saying that. Maybe he's out of the country."

"Maybe she doesn't know where he is." *Or worse,* Diamond thought, *maybe she doesn't know who he is. Maybe Mama got involved with more than one boy when she was young. Maybe that's why she's never really said much about him. Maybe that's why she ducks all my questions.*

"Maybe he can't be reached, Diamond. You'll have to ask her."

"Oh, I'll definitely be talking to her about it!"

"She'll be here soon, I'm sure. She mentioned finishing up some big work project over coffee in the cafeteria. Said a messenger's going to pick it up here."

Diamond decided to continue to press Jessica. "What's happening right now while I'm waiting?"

"What do you mean?"

"About a donor. What's happening to look for a donor?"

"Your name is being put on a national list of patients who need organs or tissue for a transplant. It's that simple. And then we wait for a matching donor."

"By the time they find one I'll probably have named all the pink bunnies."

"Hey, name one for me. That smiling bunny up at the top over there."

"The wall bunnies look alike, Jessica. I think. But the first one I name will be for you."

Jessica rolled her shoulders and worked a kink out of her neck. "I think this wing would be better off if they put up little pigs instead of bunnies. I think this hospital has gone bunny bonkers."

"Bunny bonkers, totes! But pigs? I don't think so, Jessica."

"Pigs get a lame rap, girl. They're not lazy, pigs. I mean,

what are pigs supposed to do? Aerobics? Get jobs? And they're way
smarter than dogs or horses. I read somewhere that they're as smart as
three-year-olds."

"You're pulling my chain again, Jessica."

"Not this time. Pigs are smart. And they don't wallow around
in mud to get dirty. Pigs don't sweat, so they have to keep their bodies
damp, hence the mud. I'll see if I can find the article and bring it in
for you."

"All right, I'm impressed with your pig trivia, Jessica. Still,
don't think I'd want four walls of pigs staring down at me. Shayna
would say, "Hey, they're not even kosher." And I'd have to tell her to
chill. After all, I'm climbing the walls, not eating them! Hey, do you
eat pork?"

"Not much. Especially not after reading that article and seeing
the movie Babe."

"Then, don't ever come to dinner at my grandmother's house.
Or any other Hispanic house."

Jessica slid off the bed. "Got to boogie. Work calls. See you a
little later. Okay?"

Fine. Okay.

Diamond said goodbye and settled back in the bed. She
escaped into her iPod. It was mellow, and she slowly entered outer
space and thought about pigs . . . Porky and Babe and a black and

white Arnold Ziffle. When she came back to the bunny room, she realized she was more relaxed than she'd been in days. Then she realized why. Jessica's pig talk had pulled her away from her worries about the transplant.

God, she loved that woman. *Kind of like the sister I never had.*

Diamond dozed some more, zoning out with Kanye and Jay-Z until lunch was brought in. She picked at her food and, as the tray was being removed, her mother entered the room, another coffee stain on her shirt—unsuccessfully blotted out with a napkin, little pieces of paper like confetti hanging on to show the failed effort.

"Sorry to be away so long, Niña." She kissed Diamond's cheek. "But a messenger was waiting for the work I was doing."

Her mother's face was a vivid display of weariness, eyes lined with little rivulets of pink. Diamond's pig-driven good mood vanished in a heartbeat.

"Do you even know who my father is?" Diamond had intended to talk a few pleasantries first, but the harsh question slipped out too fast.

"Y-your father? Of course I know who—"

"Then why don't you tell them about him, the doctors, the hospital? Why don't you tell them about my father? Other than 'he can't be reached.' I need a donor, Mama. And I don't want some stranger's marrow running loose in my bones when my father's marrow might be a match."

"I know, baby. But I don't have any idea where your father is or how to get in touch with him. I'm trying. I really am trying. We'll figure it out. I had to finish my project—"

"Your stupid job! I wish you'd quit! You've left me alone here, worrying about the transplant all by myself. Do you know how scary this is for me?" She swallowed the rest of her words, and after a moment added, "Sorry."

Diamond hadn't seen her mother truly bristle before. Her face clouded over with anger, red rising in her cheeks and then just as quickly disappearing. Marsha's expression softened.

"I do know how scary it is, baby, but I—"

"I'm not your baby! When are you going to learn that? When are you going to quit calling me your baby? God, I hate this hospital! It's like I friggin' live here. And most of all, I hate those stupid bunnies on the walls! And I hate that I'm always snapping at you. I love you more than anyone in the world and I'm always talking trash at you."

Neither said anything for a few minutes. Diamond glared at a spot on the wall, not wanting to glare at her mother. She listened to a muted conversation in the hall, something about a soap opera.

"Diamond, I'm sorry. I know how worried you must be. What can I do for you to make it better?"

"Do? You can find my father. You can—"

Figures in the door caused her to bite off the rest of her sentence. Dr. Goldberg and Jessica walked to the bed. Jessica stared hard at Diamond's face, and the young girl knew it was scarlet, probably angry like her mother's expression had been. Diamond worked to calm herself and touched her fingers to her cheek. Her skin was warm, and she knew it wasn't from a fever. Anger and fear had a color—red, and Diamond suspected red wasn't very becoming on her.

"Ms. Lopez, Diamond, I want to talk to you a little more on the transplant and about a donor," Dr. Goldberg said. He had an affable expression, and Diamond wondered if it was practiced, a look to seem serious, yet at the same time designed to put someone at ease.

Diamond shot an intense gaze at her mother. *My father,* she mouthed. *Tell them about my father.*

"Dr. Goldberg, I'd only briefly mentioned another possible donor before. Diamond's father."

"Yes, that would be the best possibility. But didn't you say he couldn't be reached?"

"We've been divorced for many years."

Divorced? Diamond almost snorted. *I bet you never married him. I have your last name, Mama, not his.*

"And I really have no idea how to get in touch with him. I'm trying to locate him."

"That's good, Ms. Lopez."

"But to be honest, I don't know where to start."

Dr. Goldberg stroked his chin, and Diamond wondered if he had a whole series of practiced gestures, this one to demonstrate thoughtfulness.

"In the meantime, Mrs. Lopez, Diamond has been put on the National Recipient List. When a matching donor is found there, the bone marrow will be transported here and Dr. Osborne will perform the surgery. Please be patient a minute more while I explain a few things, and then I'll answer your questions."

Diamond's patience was out the door a long time ago. Her mother held her hand and she checked an impulse to jerk it away. He droned on for some time using medical and technical terms, some of which Diamond had read in the pamphlet, others of which she suspected would end up on the list in the Scripps National Spelling Bee.

"I'll make it simple," Dr. Goldberg said as he winded down. "When a match is found, the marrow in Diamond's bones will be drained out, and then the donor's bone marrow is injected into her bloodstream."

Diamond found it easy to picture the marrow being drained. Way too easy. She imagined herself flat on her back on the operating table, legs and arms drilled with straw-like devices inserted and machines attached sucking out the marrow like you'd suck the last of a milkshake out of the bottom of the glass.

No, no, girl! Don't go there! Stay away from all the ick factors and the nightmare stuff! Think about pigs and bunnies and Mr. Bad Boy! Think only about Mr. Bad Boy in his baggies. Think about his eyes.

In frantically scanning the room to shake the image of the giant straws, her gaze settled on the mass of pink bunnies surrounding her. She imagined herself lost in a forest of real rabbits, listening to Jay-Z and wandering without care through the woods.

Papa, come find me! I need you more than ever now. Papa . . .

But as usual, there was no answer. And there was no iPod to coax her imagined father to her side or to shut out the continued explanation of the procedure.

Be careful what you wish for, girl. You wanted more information, and now you're getting it. She was into the realm of she'd rather not know. Maybe ignorance wasn't such a bad thing.

She could still hear what Dr. Goldberg was saying, but his voice seemed softer, more distant. She *did* hear him say that, after the transplant, she would have no immunity against disease and would have to live in isolation for several months. . . or up to a year!

The real live rabbits and the tranquil woods were gone in an instant. She was left with the dreadful pink wall bunnies and a gnawing hollowness in the cellar of her stomach.

"We can go over more of the details later but, first, I'd like to hear some of your questions," Dr. Goldberg finished.

"How much will it cost?" It wasn't the first thing on Diamond's mind, but it bubbled up anyway. She knew her mother's insurance wasn't going to cover everything, and she knew something like this . . . months in isolation . . . was going to have a hefty price tag.

"Not for you to worry about," her mother cut it.

"Fine. Okay," Diamond snapped. "Then how about this one: Exactly how are they going to drain my bone marrow?" Again, the image of the giant straws came to mind. "Will it hurt much? Will I be asleep?"

"You'll be asleep, Diamond. You won't feel a thing."

She noticed he didn't answer the 'how are they going to drain my bone marrow' part. In a way, she was happy he didn't answer that. Better not to know after all, she reminded herself.

"There will be a team of six in the operating room when we take your bone marrow—"

She lost the rest of his words to the imagined ca-ching of six cash registers ringing in her ears. More cash registers sounded . . . for the nurses, and then for the janitors who would sweep the floors during her stay. Ca-ching for the orderlies. Ca-ching for the dieticians and the cooks in the cafeteria and ca-ching for the—

"Will there be pink bunny wallpaper, Dr. Goldberg?"

That question clearly took Dr. Goldberg by surprise. It pretty much took Diamond by surprise, too.

"Uh, Diamond, I don't know. I have nothing to do with that kind of decision. When I leave, I think you and Jessica should spend some time together so she can counsel you on this and other related matters."

Diamond offered Dr. Goldberg an obviously insincere smile.

"I'll be around later in the week, and I'll check back with you then." He walked out without another word.

"You all right, Niña?"

"I'm fine. Okay."

"You sure?"

"Yes, I'm sure." Diamond didn't try to keep impatience out of her voice. She wished she had some of that isolation now, but in her heart knew that the last thing she wanted was to be left alone.

Jessica stepped forward. "I can stay with Diamond awhile if you have things to do, Ms. Lopez."

"Is that all right, baby girl? I can stay if you want me to."

"No, you go do what you have to. I'll be fine. Okay."

Diamond got a kiss on the cheek. Then her mother was gone.

"Teen room?"

Jessica didn't have to ask twice.

****

Their teen room visit featured purple Blue Bunny excesses and many violent, gory but sophisticated video games. Diamond won each game but one.

Finally, she softly said, "Don't know why I wigged out and asked Dr. Goldberg about bunnies."

This brought a big smile from Jessica. "No big deal. I thought it was a cool thing to say. Doctors can be way too serious sometimes. It was funny seeing him with that confused look on his face. Trouble is no one else knows our bunny secrets, from Blue Bunny to pink wall bunnies."

"What did Dr. Goldberg mean about counseling me? That sounds kind of ominous, like I'm gonna be lectured to or something."

"Girl, have I ever come close to lecturing you? I don't think so. What the doctor meant was that I should get you better prepared mentally for the bone marrow procedure."

"Mentally, Jessica? I may be too far gone for that." There she was again in the back of her mind, strapped down on a table, giant straws sucking away at her bones.

"Oh, no, Diamond. I think your mind is in fine shape. I mean, the way you function is a little . . . different than the way other peoples' minds work. You're way smarter than most kids your age. I think that's great."

"So, I'm mentally prepared?"

"As much as anybody can be for a procedure like this. Like I've told you before, concentrate on our successes. Just don't try to imagine too much. Or get too prepared."

"I won't." *Lie!* She heard the sound of giant sucking straws. Louder this time, amplified as if they were struggling to get that last drop of marrow. "And I think I'd like to go to my room. I'm a little tired."

Back in the bed, Diamond asked Jessica not to leave yet. As she sat nearby, Diamond realized that the lilac scent was stronger today.

"After our pig talk, I've been thinking about pigs, and I guess they do get a bad rap. You're the first person I ever heard defending pigs."

"Something I didn't tell you is that because donors are in such short supply, experiments are being done to study the possibility of pigs as organ and tissue donors for transplants to humans. It's quite controversial."

"Go figure!"

"In addition to, like, the moral issues, there's a possibility that pig organs or tissue could transfer diseases to humans."

"This gets better and better, Jessica. No matter how . . . *exciting* all of this might be, I don't see myself walking out of the hospital filled with pig marrow."

Jessica reached over and touched the top of Diamond's head, the lilac scent wrapping all around them. "Before you go into surgery, you have to sign a consent form that gives the surgeons the right to inject you if you start oinking or grow a pig snout."

"What?"

"Gotcha! You know I'm jerking your chain, Diamond."

After a sigh of relief, Diamond laughed. "Wow, you're a good chain-jerker Jessica! And I'll get you back. Better to be a chain-jerker than a plain old jerk, I'd say."

"Try to get some rest, and I'll drop by later." Jessica turned on *MTV Cribs* for Diamond as she left the room. "I know how much you love music videos."

"Sounds good. See you later."

"Oh, I may have a surprise for you then, too."

"Even better."

Jessica glided from the room, and Diamond snuggled back against the thin but fluffy pillows, listening to her iPod while at the same time trying to watch MTV—and slowly, her eyes closed and she began to dream.

In a dark sea of floating, glob-like cancer cells, a light emerged from the center of the muck, growing lighter and stronger as it spread out in all directions.

Under it, on a stainless steel table, cold to the touch, six green-clad doctors placed Diamond. There was a whirr of machinery, the hiss of some oxygen contraption, but those sounds were soon overpowered by the driving, more pleasant beat of Jay-Z's latest hit. Beyoncé crooned, too, competing with it and creating a wonderful cacophony. The light started strobing to it.

The light became so powerful that it overtook the evil cancer cells and turned them to dust one by one, and replaced each with a glowing orb of white light. Nuyorican Knockout was working her magic.

Diamond wasn't going to need those giant metal straws to suck the marrow out of her bones. Nuyorican Knockout was going to make sure that no one else's marrow—and no pig marrow—found its way inside her bootilicious fourteen-year-old body.

Nuyorican Knockout was going to do what all the doctors and research scientists couldn't . . . find a cure for the dreaded lymphoblastic leukemia.

Nuyorican Knockout was going to prevail.

But, in some part of Diamond's mind, she knew that wasn't going to happen.

****

Diamond pretended to be asleep. Marsha sat in the far corner of the small room, hand cupped over the cell phone, trying to keep the conversation muted. Diamond still managed to pick up enough of it. Her mother had hit another dead end in trying to find her father.

So, at least Marsha knew the man, Diamond realized. She wasn't the product of a forgotten liaison with some nameless, faceless high school hunk that her mother had just happened to hook up with for a one-nighter.

Through squinted eyes, Diamond watched her mother sip coffee that was probably cold by now. It was like she was mainlining caffeine.

She made another call, talking to someone named Felicia, someone Diamond didn't know.

"Don't you remember Larry?" Marsha asked. "Larry Levin?"

BINGO! Diamond's father had a last name.

"Yeah, that Larry," Marsha continued. "He used to hang out at the Blind Pig—"

More pig talk, Diamond thought.

"—and drink beer with the cops who got off-duty. Yeah, he had that smile."

Diamond strained to hear more, but obviously this "Felicia" was taking a turn talking. She spied Marsha sipping more coffee.

"Thanks anyway," Marsha said. "I guess I'm just going to have to go downtown and visit Larry's old haunts. Maybe someone there will remember my drug- and drink-abusing ex." Softer: "I wonder if anyone there will remember me?"

****

Diamond glided through her weekend on the high from Jessica's Friday afternoon visit and her big surprise, which was the best surprise in the entire world. Jessica had somehow convinced "the powers that be" to let Adam visit one more time.

It wouldn't necessarily happen right away, Jessica had said, but that didn't matter as much as the fact that he was coming. Diamond was grateful that the fear and awkwardness of that first kiss was over. That first kiss was totes—what that fantastically hot boy's lips could do!

It would be sweeter still if they could get a little lip-locking time alone together. But Diamond could think of no way to keep the room free of nurses, unless she stationed Jessica outside the door as a security guard. She suspected that the nurses wouldn't be happy about being barred from the room, but the happiness of hospital personnel wasn't her problem.

As much as she wanted to see Adam, she was a little bit glad he couldn't visit right this moment. She felt weaker than usual, and she didn't want to see him like this . . . her doing a great impersonation of a limp dishrag. It was nice to have something to look forward to though.

Her iPod continued to help her get through long stretches of time as she escaped into her special music-inspired dream world. But one morning after another barely-touched breakfast of what the hospital tried to pass off as scrambled eggs, she listened to *Rent* for the umpteenth million time. Her father's voice interrupted the music.

"So, you're on the waiting list for a transplant, corazón. A big step toward getting back into dancing shape."

"I guess so, Papa. Some days it seems like I'll never be able to dance again. Like today. I can barely sit up. I don't want to think about getting out of this bed to use the bathroom. I'm afraid I'll collapse. And the idea of someone else's marrow in my bones gives me a kind of icky feeling. It would be great if I could use your marrow. That would really seal the deal."

"Hey, at least it won't be a pig's marrow."

"Yeah, there is that. I won't have Babe or Arnold Ziffle in my bloodstream. Papa, I've been thinking about you playing the guitar and not being able to make a living that way. Which is cool. But I was wondering what kind of work you do that lets you drive a Porsche."

Silence lingered.

"Papa?"

"I'm still here. It's hard to describe my work. Some of it is confidential. But I've been very successful with it. And when you get out of here, I'll be able to take you dancing any place you want to go. Not just New York, corazón. London, Paris, Rio. And . . ."

A nurse was walking toward the bed.

"No, Papa, don't go!"

But he was gone.

Diamond glared at the nurse who was taking her blood

pressure, but the woman glanced away at the monitor, paying her no

attention and not saying a word.

Washington Street

"Not on wheels, Jessica. Never on wheels."

Diamond refused to be transported to the teen room in a wheelchair as Jessica had suggested, but she did let Jessica help her as they walked slowly down the hall, one hand in hers, the other gripping a railing that ran along the wall. The wood was smooth and cool to the touch, heavily lacquered, and Diamond wondered if despite all the disinfectants . . . the smell of which filled the hallway . . . there weren't germs tap dancing all over the railing.

She'd read that the first one hundred days after a transplant were key, both in determining if host versus grafts disease was present and if the patient had a good chance in general of making it. Germs could be a killer. Graft versus host attacked the liver, skin, basically a person's guts, the lungs. She could get real bad inflammation in her intestines, severe diarrhea, nausea, vomiting, abdominal pain. She could feel so bad she wished she were dead.

"Even after this transplant I don't want to be on wheels, Jessica." And even after the transplant she wouldn't want to stay in that suffocating bed.

In fact, one more minute in that pink bunny room and she would've gnawed through her arm in frustration and boredom. God, she hated the bunny prison. And that's what it was—a colorful flower-filled jail cell that kept her away from her friends and school and away from Abuela's air freshener bedecked apartment, away from her own room festooned with its big posters, away from the sounds of the neighborhood and the clackity-clack of the subway, which was its own music.

"Wheelchairs aren't a bad thing, Diamond. They were invented just to help people get around."

Diamond shrugged off Jessica's comment.

There were always people in the teen room in wheelchairs, but they weren't big booty Nuyorican superheroes who were once dancing fools.

"What do you want to do first, Diamond? A little Blue Bunny to start?"

"Yeah, I guess so. I'm up for trying one."

But one taste of the sweet frozen concoction and Diamond had her fill. None of the games much interested her either. She found it hard to concentrate.

"Enough of these festivities," she announced after a short while. "I want to go back to my jail cell."

Jessica gave her a half-smile. "We'll take it slow. Lunch should be there by the time we get back."

"Will the gourmet delights never end?"

Jessica chattered all the way back to the room, but she mostly talked to herself, mentioning her aunt and a planned trip to visit her in the next few days. Diamond wanted her to shut up—along with the orderlies who were talking about some soap opera again. She almost told Jessica to shut up and leave her alone. Once in bed, though, Diamond didn't want Jessica to leave.

While Diamond ignored her lunch, she and Jessica talked about music, dancing, and movies, even dishing about the nurse who had taken her blood pressure during Adam's visit.

"She didn't even say 'hello.' Looked like her face was as starched as her dress."

Mostly Diamond did the dishing, but Jessica did say that particular nurse wasn't exactly the patients' favorite.

Diamond slept awhile and, when her mother came back and accidentally woke her up, she saw that the veins were redder in her watery eyes.

"Mama, how much sleep are you getting?"

"Sleep? Oh, that would cut into my coffee-drinking time. No, I'm okay. I'm fine. How are you feeling?"

Fine. Okay.

Diamond shrugged. "*Carpe diem*, and other Latin stuff like that. Anything happening on the donor front?"

Marsha hesitated. "Not that I know of. They said it might be a long wait."

"They were right. Oh, Mama, I'm so sick of all this waiting and not knowing anything. And look how much time is passing . . . school's almost out, only a few weeks left of it. Do you realize how long I've been here? How much school I missed?"

That's something else that had been niggling at the back of Diamond's mind . . . school. Not only was she missing her friends and all the activities there, the sounds of lockers slamming, students laughing, and the squeak of shoes on the gymnasium floor . . . she was missing her studies. There'd been no talk of the Tutor from Hell, or of her doing any schoolwork for that matter. Here she was fourteen . . . not far off from fifteen . . . and in the eighth grade, most of her friends a year younger because she'd been held back once from lymphoblastic leukemia. When . . . if . . . the transplant happened, she could be isolated for up to a year. She clearly remembered Dr. Goldberg saying that. She'd be fifteen . . . not far off from sixteen . . . and heading into her freshman year in high school. God, she might be able to drive before she went to high school. She'd be older than everybody! Well, older than her classmates. Mr. Bad Boy was probably her age . . . he looked her age . . . but he'd be a year ahead.

At this rate, she'd be twenty before she got her diploma!

Tears started pouring over Diamond's cheeks, and they tasted salty on her lips. She couldn't control them anymore—and didn't want to.

"Oh, baby girl. I am so sorry all of this is happening to you. I'd trade places with you if I could."

Diamond allowed herself to be wrapped up tightly in her mother's embrace. But her whole body heaved as she shed tears until she was exhausted. If only she really was a big booty Nuyorican superhero.

Finally Diamond fell back into the pillows. She didn't think she'd ever be able to lift herself up again.

Why would she want to?

To escape those wack bunnies surrounding her? The bunnies would probably be the last thing she ever saw. Diamond closed her eyes and still she saw the bunnies. They danced around the room, elephants doing the mambo joining them. She realized her mother was holding her hand. *Don't let go, Mama,* she wanted to say, but the effort to open her mouth didn't seem worthwhile. Her stomach churned as if filled with rotting food that had come to life, animated like zombie bits and determined to crawl up her throat. She ached with a different kind of pain that seemed to emanate from her bones. She didn't know how long she endured the ordeal, but it finally passed and she fell into a deep sleep.

Nuyorican Knockout tugged Diamond up on her swag surfer, and they tipped their faces up to the sun. Late spring, it was pleasantly warm, and the breeze felt good playing across their skin.

"Where to?" Nuyorican asked her.

The superhero rarely talked to Diamond.

"A place called the Blind Pig. It's a bar or something like it."

"Easy to find," Nuyorican said.

Diamond figured Nuyorican could find any place in the city.

Nuyorican nudged the controls and the swag surfer shot away from the bunny prison—somehow Diamond had gotten out through the window this time— and they rocketed above the streets so fast that the colors of the cars below blurred into streaks resembling chalk drawings in the park that ran together in the rain.

The noises were intoxicating—the bleats of taxi

horns, the barks of street vendors, music spilling out

of this window and that door . . . blues, jazz, hip-hop,

moldy rock, even easy-listening elevator crap. God,

someone was playing country-western. Diamond closed

her ears and concentrated on the smells . . . hot dogs

and sauerkraut, pretzels, the stink of garbage left on the

curbs and in the alleys, the scent of flowers rising from

baskets hanging from eaves and fire escapes and street

poles. Everything was better and brighter away from

her prison.

"Where are we going?" Diamond asked.

Somehow, her voice carried above the whistling wind

and all the other sounds.

"Washington Street," Nuyorican answerd.

"The Blind Pig is on Washington. It's not the best

neighborhood."

Diamond wasn't worried about that. Nuyorican

could take on anything and anybody in the worst

neighborhood. Diamond was, however, worried that

she might not wake up from this dream. When she

slept, it was for hours, and it seemed like it was getting

harder and harder to wake up. It would just be so easy

to sleep forever.

They landed on a sidewalk and, with a gesture, the swag surfer disappeared to some pocket dimension. Diamond and Nuyorican walked along an oddly deserted West Village street. Time blurred and then they were walking down the stairs and into a smoky bar.

Hadn't some law been passed somewhere to make all these places non-smoking?

The bouncer greeted Nuyorican, seeming not to notice Diamond . . . good thing, she thought, as she wasn't old enough to be here. The raucous talk, laughter, music and stale air slammed at her. Together, she and Nuyorican fought their way to the bar.

"I haven't seen Larry, pretty lady," the barkeep said. "Not for a few days. I assume that's what you're here for . . . Larry Levine."

Nuyorican nodded.

"What'll you have?"

"A Diet Coke."

Diamond knew Nuyorican wouldn't drink alcohol. It might dull the superhero's senses, and then she'd have a hard time piloting the swag surfer back to the hospital.

"Larry's been going to AA, says he's been off

drugs for two years. So you might not recognize him."

Of course she and Nuyorican wouldn't recognize him . . . they'd never seen him. But Diamond knew he would be good looking and would have dark hair and dark eyes.

"Not as selfish as he used to be, either. He bought a round for some friends week before last. Gave me a tip, too."

Certainly he'd have money for that, Diamond almost shouted. He drives a Porsche.

Nuyorican sipped the drink.

Diamond thought it was a good thing this was a dream because she saw the menu posted behind the bar . . . a Diet Coke, any kind of soft drink . . . was seven dollars.

The barkeep started talking to a skinny man wearing a crushed hat. He was almost as skinny as Diamond.

Nuyorican drained the glass and set it on the bar, nodded to Diamond, and gestured at the door to leave. Diamond didn't want to go. She didn't much care for these surroundings, but there were no pink bunnies, and no elephants danced the mambo. The music was all right.

Nuyorican tugged her.

The skinny man turned to stare at them.

"You looking for me, lady?"

"I hardly think so," Nuyorican answered.

"It's me. Larry."

Nuyorican pinned him to the bar. "Your bone marrow," she hissed.

Rarely had Diamond heard her talk, and never had she heard Nuyorican use that tone.

"My bone marrow? I'll have to think about it," Larry said. He wasn't intimidated one bit by the big booty superhero. "That might hurt some, giving up my marrow. I'll have to think hard."

****

Since Diamond spent most of her time in her room, she decided to make peace with the pink bunnies. At times, she even found herself talking to them out loud. "Too wack," she told Jessica one sunny morning. "Talking to them out loud, I mean."

"Wack is when they start talking back to you. Better let me know if that happens."

Diamond almost laughed, but managed to stop herself. Instead, she smiled. Smiling felt good, and she didn't do it very often anymore. It was like exercising muscles that hadn't been used in a long time.

The pain in her bones had diminished, and the nausea was nearly gone. It was the meds they were giving her, she knew, and they were so strong that they had to be used sparingly. She couldn't understand why she had to wait in the hospital all this time while they looked for a donor. Why couldn't she go back to Abuela's? She could wait there.

"It's because of the pain meds," Jessica explained. "You're on some pretty strong stuff and it wouldn't be safe to keep you at home where the nurses can't monitor you. We don't want you to pass out again, and we need to make sure you're getting enough nutrition. Besides, I've gotten to know your grandmother, and she'd be a constant worried wreck looking after you."

Diamond grumbled. She knew it was true, but she hated it.

"Up to visiting the teen room yet?"

"Not quite yet." Well, she was feeling up to it, but she didn't want to go. She wanted to lay right here and wallow in her self-poured tub of pity.

"How about watching TV? Almost time for some reruns." Jessica picked up a TV Guide. "Green Acres?"

Arnold Ziffle. Diamond had enough pig thoughts.

Diamond shook her head. "Not now, Jessica. I'm still feeling like a rerun myself."

"Want me to leave, so you can zone out?"

"No, please stay. I'm getting wigged out at where my mind goes when I'm alone too long. Just stay for a little bit. I'm sure I'll doze off soon . . . again . . . and you can sneak out then."

"How about some more tats?"

"I'm tattooed out. Sorry to be a drag. When I feel halfway decent, I really want to, you know, do things and have fun. The idea of more tattoos . . . real ones, actually . . . is exciting, but—"

A soft chime cut Diamond off. Jessica looked to a pager on her waist. "I need to step out for a minute, Diamond, but I'll be right back. Don't go anywhere."

"Yeah, like I could go anywhere."

Jessica's parting comment brought on another smile, but this one hurt her face. "Am I the girl who can't smile because it pains me too much?" she asked the bunnies.

They didn't answer.

She lay back and closed her eyes. She'd been sleeping a lot the past few days, but it hadn't been good sleep. It had been wake-up-every-few-minutes-sleep. Jump at some sound from out in the hall. Strain to hear an ambulance coming in. Strain harder to pick up the honk of fire trucks. And then there was the hiss and purr of monitors in this room, the gentle "bleep" of equipment in other rooms.

And then when she finally had a good snooze going, some nurse came to wake her up and take her blood pressure. Whatever her "numbers" were, they were meaningless. She was meaningless in the overall scheme of things. There might not be a tomorrow for her.

Don't think about it. I have today. That's all that matters. Today.

And her life wasn't completely meaningless, was it? She remembered the men commenting on her booty when she walked to school in the mornings. It seemed like a hundred years ago. And she remembered kissing Adam.

Yeah, put that on my gravestone . . . AT LEAST SHE KISSED ADAM. That's something else that'll cost mom, a funeral, casket... insurance won't cover a dime of that. She'll be in debt up to her eyeballs.

Diamond wasn't sure if she dozed off, but she heard a noise and had a sense of waking up. She yawned, opened her eyes, and stifled a scream.

Beside the bed stood a giant pink bunny.

Diamond tried to scoot back in the bed to escape it, but there was nowhere to go.

Hey, wait a minute! A pink bunny wearing lilac perfume? I don't think so.

"Well, well, if it isn't Jessica Bunny. God, girl, you scared me silly there for a minute. But I love it! Please don't take it off."

"You should smile all the time, Diamond. You have this special kind of smile that sparkles. I guess your mother named you Diamond when she discovered how you shine so bright. You could light up the darkest room!"

Then, a voice from the doorway cried, "My God, what is that thing?"

Diamond looked around the giant pink bunny to see her mother standing at the door, hand at her mouth as though to cover a shriek.

"Hi, Mama. This is a visiting relative of the wall bunnies. Say hello to Jessica Bunny."

"Jessica?"

"It's me, Ms. Lopez. Hope I didn't freak you out. But you see, Diamond and I have this thing about bunnies. It's kind of hard to explain. I found this bunny costume. I tried to find a pig, but those were all rented."

"Anything that makes my baby girl smile that wide is great."

"Now that you're back, Ms. Lopez, I think I'll run on. See you later, Diamond. I'm starting to sweat in this."

When Jessica left, Diamond curled up a little. Her strength was beginning to desert her again. She faced toward the wall.

Marsha sat down on the end of the bed. "Damn Larry," she whispered.

****

Diamond paced, slowly. She did everything slowly these days, one hand out always ready to catch her if her knobby knees started to get too wobbly.

The strong meds were still keeping the aches and nausea away. . . and God knew what else they were doing to her. Could she be addicted to them? Would it matter if she was addicted to them?

She glanced at the door. Adam was coming through it.

"I've missed you so much, Diamond." He said it like he really meant it, and his smile reached his eyes. It was warm and inviting and chased away thoughts of the strong medicine.

"I've missed you too, Adam."

It was like a dream.

He threw his arms around her and hugged her so tight it hurt a little. Then they were kissing. *Oh, God, those lips! His scent! His arms! Don't let this ever ever ever end!*

They kissed for a long time, and when they stopped, they simply stood there gazing into each other's eyes and talking quietly about school almost out and about the hospital, Jessica's bunny costume, Storm from *The X-Men*, and Abuela's air freshener collection.

Diamond was reluctant to ask Adam how he was spending his time. She was afraid he might mention the skank.

Another kiss ended their chit-chat, and this kiss was even more awesome. Adam started stroking her head. "I love your hair. It's grown back like silk." He whispered the words, his breath warm in her ear.

Was this what love felt like?

She took his hand, led him across the room, and they sat on the side of the bed.

"Diamond, do you have access to a computer? Like, for email or to check out Facebook and stuff?"

Diamond pulled a face. "I used to. Unfortunately, I don't have one right now. The one my mom's boss was letting me use had to go back to the office. There's one in the teen room, but it's ancient and it's a real pain to get online. Takes forever to load pages. It's so annoying. And there's always somebody else using it."

"Well, yeah, maybe it's better this way. You know, conserve your energy, and lay back and rest."

"Yeah, I guess so."

"You really need to rest."

He was right, she supposed. But she was always resting, whether she wanted to or not.

There was something in his voice, his attitude, the way he said "rest." It didn't sound very positive. Something felt weird. She couldn't put her finger on it, but it was a creepy feeling.

Adam put his arm around Diamond's shoulders, and Diamond loved being hugged against his solid chest, adoring his ravishing scents. What was that fragrance? Bod? The one they advertised at the movie theater? She turned up her face, parting her lips ever so slightly. Her heart was beating like a berserk metronome.

She anticipated another kiss, but Adam had other things in mind. His hand touched her throat, the fingers lingering there, and then drifted lower. Oh, God! She was so not ready for *this! Lots of heavy kissing, for sure! Petting . . . no boy had done that to her yet. Help!*

Do the math, girl. Do the math. Your mom's thirty. You're fourteen. She was sixteen when she had you, maybe fifteen when she got pregnant. So, mom had to have been into some heavy petting at this age, maybe younger. Girls my age do this. Girls younger than me do this. Adora is a year younger than me. But I don't want to do this. . . not yet.

She said nothing, trying to think what that skank Adora would do. No, she well knew what Adora would do. Or what a big booty Nuyorican super girl would do! In her mind, she searched for an image of Nuyorican Knockout, but everything was blank. She could think of nothing but the way his hands felt on her. She was at a complete loss about how to react to this new development, and she instinctively twisted a little, denying him what he wanted.

Adam's hand slid away. "Sorry, Diamond, didn't mean to freak you out."

Her incipient reply was smothered by his lips, and the incident was quickly forgotten as the kiss went on and on until a nurse came in and unceremoniously ended the visit.

Adam had been gone less than five minutes when Diamond's energy and enthusiasm fled—as though something huge and nasty had chased them away. There was a buzzing in her head, like a beehive. Was she going to have some sort of fainting spell?

No way, girl. No buzzing. No beehive. Embrace the unknown! Carpe diem!

Diamond sat up in the bed, propped against the pillows. She so wanted to see Jessica, tell her about Adam's visit. Go down to the teen room, like old times. She thought she could well manage the teen room right now . . . the meds were keeping her going . . . but maybe they were also responsible for the buzzing.

As though listening in the hall, Jessica materialized in the door and was followed into the room by a nurse and Dr. Goldberg.

"Diamond, we are in luck. We've found three possible matches from the donor base. Three! One of them is bound to work out!" Dr. Goldberg said. He spoke loudly and with more enthusiasm than she'd heard him use before. "We'll be doing some tests to find out which is the closest match. With luck, you'll have new, healthy marrow in a day or two."

"That fast?"

"Fast? Haven't you been in this hospital long enough?"

****

One day later, he was back in her room, eyes bright and hands rubbing together. "We're going to get started right away, so they'll start prepping you right now."

"Now?"

"Right now. No reason to wait."

"That's way great news. Who's the donor? Can I meet her? What do you mean by prepping me? When do we start? How long will it take?"

Dr. Goldberg was practically beaming. "The donor has requested to remain anonymous. So, I'm sorry that we can't give out that information. You see, Diamond, there are a lot of celebrities who try to help with things like this, professional football players, movie stars, we even have a few musicians on the list. Black, white, rich, powerful, odd ducks, too. They don't want the publicity, they get enough of it as is. So . . . some folks keep their names out of this."

"Football marrow," Diamond mused.

"As far as your prep goes, it will involve a few days of chemo, to make sure the cancer's gone. Then we begin removing your bone marrow, which as you know from reading the booklets, contains the chemicals that make your immunities strong. Without those chemicals, you're vulnerable to every germ in the book, so that's why you have to be isolated until the new bone marrow gets established in your body. It's great news that we've found a donor. This is exciting! Try to relax."

Relax?

It was exciting. So exciting she knew she couldn't possibly relax. Musician marrow? Classical. She bet it was some classical pianist rather than a rap artist. God, wouldn't it be awesome sauce if she had Beyoncé marrow?

And it was also scary.

As the doctor walked out, yet another nurse came in with a cart and a stand for infusions.

"I wish I knew who my donor is. I hate to admit it, but I'm frightened, Jessica. Is this going to hurt? Please tell me it's not going to hurt." A pause. "Tell me the truth, though."

Jessica held both of Diamond's hands. "For a few days, they'll be mostly administering chemotherapy. That won't hurt a bit."

"I've been there before."

"Yes, so you know what to expect. Except that this round will be much stronger and more intense."

"So this won't be a lot of laughs."

"Not many, I'm afraid. It won't hurt, but—"

"I'll be seriously nauseous. That's hurting, you know."

"Look at it this way, Diamond. Each day of treatment is a day closer to the transplant. Oh, one other thing. Prior to the conditioning, they'll insert a small catheter into a vein right above your heart."

"It truly gets better and better," Diamond mocked.

"This *is* better, girl. The catheter lets them administer drugs and take blood samples without having to stick needles into your arms and hands."

Jessica glanced at the nurses. "Time for me to boogie on out of here and let them get on with it."

"Please—don't stay away too long, Jessica. Jessica Bunny. Maybe come back in the bunny suit?"

"Maybe." She stepped toward the door.

"Where's my mother? Why isn't she here? Does she know about the donor? Does she know about all this additional chemo?"

"She's on her way. She should be here any minute. She was in the cafeteria slugging down that coffee she's hooked on."

Jessica walked out, and Diamond muttered, "Show time."

The nurses stared at her.

They're not going to be any fun.

Diamond asked for her iPod, let the music take her away, closed her eyes, and desperately tried not to pay attention to what was happening.

After four days of chemo, as she was being wheeled into the operating room to have her bone marrow sucked out, Diamond was weaker and more emaciated. She hurt in places she didn't know she had.

"Death will have a hard act to follow," she mused.

At least this wasn't going to hurt, the transplant. Or so she had been told. She'd be out cold. Oblivion. They'd all mentioned that she'd be unconscious through the whole thing.

Oh, yeah, I can so go there. Oblivion City. Beyoncé marrow singing through my bones.

When she woke up in the recovery room, it was over, and she hardly hurt at all. But the aching grew. So they'd lied . . . a little . . . it wasn't wholly painless after all. She hurt a little, a soft throb that suffused her. In the distance, she could hear Peter Rosenberg on HOT 97 FM introduce "Woke Up" by Big Sean. She started jamming to the lyric, "Thank God I woke up," off his mixtape, *Detroit*. Once again, hip-hop carried her through the moment.

They'd stuck needles into her hip bones and taken out the marrow. No skin punctures, no incisions, no stitches. She was told that Tylenol would take care of what aches there were.

They were right. The Tylenol worked.

Two days later, the transplant took place . . . in Diamond's room, as she was surprised to learn. There was no surgery, not in an operating room with those huge glaring lights and all the machines whirring away. Nothing like on *House* and the other TV shows, nothing like she'd expected.

She'd just assumed it would be a real big procedure.

The donor's bone marrow was simply infused into Diamond's

bloodstream the way any blood product might be. Her mother, Abuela and Jessica were there—looking like extras in a science-fiction movie because of the hospital attire and surgical masks.

"Wow. That was a walk in the park," she said to Jessica. She looked over at the wallpaper. "Right, dudes? Or should I say a 'hop' in the park? If I have basketball player marrow, I should be able to jump higher than all of you."

Two nurses glanced at the wallpaper, then each other.

"It's our version of bunny humor," Jessica explained.

Dr. Goldberg said that the next two to four weeks would be the most critical because the high-dose chemo had treated her bone marrow, thus crippling her body's immune system. Diamond's world would now be inhabited only by people in gowns, caps, and surgical masks. She was kept pumped full of antibiotics and blood transfusions. Daily blood samples were taken.

Within a day of the transplant, Diamond developed such excessive symptoms of a severe case of flu that she didn't want any visitors. Why would she want anyone to just sit there watching her suffer with vomiting, diarrhea, nausea, fever, and extreme weakness?

"Like the flu on steroids," she said one day to no one in particular, because she was often unaware whether or not there were people in the room. The ever faithful pink bunnies were always there, though. She worried about the host versus grafts thing.

Her world had been whittled down to the simple and dreadful routine of fever and chills, vomiting and reaching desperately for the bed pan she was usually too weak to lift.

And only five days had passed.

Then a week went by, then ten days.

It was a roller-coaster ride of feeling much better one day and like death-warmed-over the next. At about the three-week mark, the roller-coaster began to level off, finally seeming like a train running on a level track.

"This means the donor marrow is engrafting itself and producing healthy cells in your body," Dr. Goldberg said. "If there's another week showing this kind of progress, you can go home—at least, for the time being. You'll still have to come back for tests, and you may have to stay here longer."

Home! Her own bedroom. Her real life! Visitors. Tamara and Shayna. Sadie and Jude, with their cousinly treats. But most of all, Adam! Endless Adam.

I'll be ecstatic if he and Adora aren't married by now.

"But you'll have to seriously limit visitors. No pets. Everything extremely clean. No going out," he said. "No going out for a very long time."

Her heart sank, and she once again recalled him mentioning up to a year.

I'll be able to drive before I can go to high school.

The day before Diamond was to be released, she was dozing fitfully when Jessica woke her to give her one sweet getting-out-of-the-hospital gift: a Swarovski Crystal pig and two piglets! This special gesture brought tears to Diamond's eyes.

She was wheeled out of the hospital the next morning.

****

Going back to school in the Fall was out of the question, but the Tutor from Hell would return. And her only forays out of the apartment were for visits to the hospital for monitoring and blood transfusions.

Visitors were indeed limited—to family only at first, and they had to wear caps, gowns and masks. Diamond was allowed to text and make phone calls, but usually felt too lousy to do so. And she rapidly realized how small this room was next to her hospital room. Not that its size mattered at first, since she spent almost all of her time in bed.

But slowly, steadily, she felt better and got her strength back.

Abuela did everything she could to fatten her up. She cooked Diamond's favorites, and there was always a piece of *tres leches* cake available. Diamond could feel the black beans and rice starting to ooze out of her ears.

In her first text with Tamara and Shayna, Diamond was nervous and didn't know what to text. But in less than a minute, they were all chatting away happily.

LiDiamond:
hi are u there

CUtamara:
hey girl welcome home to your crib we love ya

LiDiamond:
:) !!!!!

CUtamara:
is abuela makin u phat yet

LiDiamond:
lol i could only hope.

CUtamara:
dats aight.

LiDiamond:
u da bomb

CUtamara:
we can't wait to hang wit ya

LiDiamond:
me too da 3 chicateers forever

CUtamara:
lol

They had been texting for several minutes when Diamond realized they hadn't mentioned Adam, and that caused her to be too worried to ask about him. Her mood took a nose dive as every worst fear paraded through her mind.

CUtamara:
hey girl u still there?

LiDiamond:
wat o yea totes.

CUtamara:
when can we see u?

> **LiDiamond:**
> ya can't wait to see u either. when can you dudes get up here?

They decided on the day after tomorrow. Diamond was miserable as she moped around the apartment. She wanted to get some inside information about Adam, but they hadn't they mentioned him, not even once. *Why?*

She decided to text them right back, then changed her mind. She couldn't face what she knew would probably be bad news. All she could do was lose herself with Maroon 5, Jay-Z, Beyoncé and Kanye West. God, but she needed to get some new CDs. Did she have Beyoncé marrow? Or marrow from some Italian opera singer? A classical pianist? A violist? Beyoncé, she decided finally.

Despite her down feelings about Adam, Diamond was feeling better in a completely new way. Since the transplant, she'd felt whole . . . complete . . . hard to explain exactly, but as though some missing part had been added to whatever made up Diamond Lopez.

Several afternoons later, she was on the couch with her music, a generous slice of *tres leches* cake and a glass of guava juice when the doorbell rang. She was alone, her mom at work, Albuela at the store, and so she answered it.

She plodded over and opened the door and there stood Adam!

He was smiling, stepping toward her. She returned the smile, her heart thumping as she anticipated his kiss. But then a jolt of warning flashed over her. She bolted back.

"No! Don't come any closer, Adam."

"Diamond, have I done something wrong? Are you mad at me?"

"Oh, no, Adam. Wait here. I'll be right back."

Diamond dressed in her cap, gown and mask, finding an unused set which she carried to Adam.

"Got to put these on before you come in. I'm not supposed to be exposed to any germs. Welcome to my sanitized world." Briefly, she explained the need for this special outfit.

They sat on the couch a few feet apart. Adam seemed stiff, unsure what to do.

A long silence.

Diamond tried to come up with something witty and appropriate to say, but her brain was on overdrive. She could think of nothing other than, "This sucks."

Adam stood up. "Maybe I better come back another time."

Diamond pulled herself to her feet. "No, please don't go, Adam. I'm sorry this is so awkward. We have to keep our distance because of my wack immune system, but all I want to do is sit next to you and kiss you! This really sucks! But I've come so far . . . from leukemia . . . a bone marrow transplant . . . I can't let it all be undone."

Diamond started to reach out for his hand, but remembered the gloves. She wasn't laughing anymore. "I know this is awful Adam. But it won't last long. Oh, God, I so want to kiss you!"

"I want to kiss you too, Diamond. Maybe we should sit back down and talk."

They sat on the couch.

They talked.

She answered his questions about the hospital, the bone marrow transplant and medicine she had to take, about this being her best chance but no real guarantee, her fears about the future. He listened compassionately, but Diamond sensed something about Adam was different.

They soon got around to talking about computers, emails and Facebook, and Diamond just had to ask, "Adam, in the hospital, you talked about emails and Facebook in this kind of . . . curious way. I had a feeling there was a lot more that you weren't saying. Please tell me what it is."

"Well . . . if you really want to know. It's Adora. Girl's like totally out of control since she learned about cyber bullying."

"Huh?"

"She's a cyber bully."

Diamond had heard about cyber bullying, where skanks . . . apparently like Adora . . . post way nasty things about someone on social networks like Facebook. There was no way to stop it, was there? Freedom of speech and all of that.

"So she's posting stuff about me, isn't she?"

"Look—"

"What's she been saying, Adam?"

"I only saw the first few. But I heard about others. I tried to talk her out of it, but she refused, and then I quit reading them. Supposedly they've gotten even nastier. I have nothing to do with her anymore. Nothing to say to her. It's just wrong."

"And what was that first one? That she posted . . ."

"Dia—"

"I have to know, Adam. Believe me, not knowing is way worse." She hated this conversation, but it was important to her, and she loved how honest he was being with her.

"Alright, if you really have to know. She pretty much said, 'What leukemia poster child was kicked out of school for being grossly sick and contagious? She's in an institution, bald, skinny and way pitiful.' Something like that."

"And they got worse than that?" A kind of fever crawled over Diamond from head to foot, and a sudden, immature rage welled up from the pit of her stomach. She felt hollow, totally debilitated and utterly helpless.

"Diamond, I don't know how to. . ."

"It's okay. I asked. My fault for pushing. But I don't want to hear any more."

Actually, she did want to hear a lot more, like why he liked Adora to begin with and if the skank was still his girlfriend, and if they were still sucking each other's faces in the stairwell, and why he'd hang out with Adora if he disapproved of her cyberbullying so much. And did he really mean it when he said that he is having nothing to do with her. She did hear that right, didn't she? That he is having nothing to do with Toxic Adora. There were so many questions!

Nuyorican Knockout was screaming, "How could she be your shawty, Mr. Bad Boy . . . why? How could that so-called female slither into your heart? She better have slithered right out."

As Diamond looked at Adam, she noticed that one area of his face appeared to glow from his beautiful soul and the other side seemed almost devious… the side of him that was attracted to Adora. What did he see in that skank anyway? What did any of the boys she sucked face with see in her? Maybe she was just . . . easy.

Nuyorican Knockout slammed Adora's evil face into a wall as she continued to shout in a voice painful in its intensity, "You hurt me, but you will never hurt me

again! Your cyber bullying hurt me! But I am immune

to your pitiful words."

Adam interrupted Diamond's thoughts.

"All the things you went through, the bone marrow transplant, all the chemo. It's like out of a movie, so unreal. You're brave, Diamond. The bravest person I know. One thing I was wondering . . . who was your donor?"

"I was told the person wanted to be anonymous. It was a condition for donating the marrow. Guess I'll never know. I'd like to think it was some rap star rather than a quarterback."

Diamond realized that she had slid down some on the couch. She was so debilitated, she had trouble sitting up. Adam reached over to try to support her head.

"Diamond, I've got to go now. It's a long way home on the train. You don't mind if I come by again, do you? When can I see you again?"

Every day, was the first thought that came to her, but it wasn't what she said. "Let me call you. It'll be, like, in a day or two. Count on it. I definitely want you to come back."

As they walked to the door, Adam held her gloved hand. They lingered, looking into each other's eyes. Diamond so wanted to rip off their masks. With a final but gentle squeeze, he simply took of the borrowed hospital garments and left.

Best hand squeeze I've ever had. Oh yeah, I'm livin' large.
Awesome sauce.

Diamond collapsed onto her bed, trying not to think about
Adora and what she might be writing on Facebook. She was too
exhausted to listen to music. Slowly, mercifully, she drifted off into a
dreamless sleep.

The next day she felt physically better, but isolated and out of
touch with the whole world. Everyone dressed in a gown, cap, and
mask gave her walls-closing-in world a constant sci-fi aura.

Diamond pigged out on *tres leches* cake and guava juice
when she wasn't escaping into her music and dreams. Tamara and
Shayna visited a couple of times and told her more about Adora's
rude comments, and Diamond's rage was made even worse by her
inability to do anything to protect or defend herself. Meantime, they
joked about Diamond's sci-fi world and enjoyed each other's company,
but after a few weeks there were fewer visits, only phone calls, and
eventually those too began to slack off. It was the height of summer,
after all, and Diamond imagined that they were at the pool, or sitting
on some sunny bleacher watching a softball game.

Adam continued to visit too—for a while.

Adam and Diamond were able to laugh about the *Twilight*
Zone quality of Diamond's life, and they took lots of pleasure in

merely being able to look into each other's eyes. But soon even his
visits tapered off, and so did the texts and phone calls. He always
had a reasonable excuse, but Diamond's fears about Adam and Adora
blossomed, as though fed a huge dose of vitamins.

She knew that her mother had months ago broken it off with
Michael . . . Adam's father. She was disappointed in a way. When
she'd been really really sick, she hadn't wanted to share her mother.
Now she realized it was past time her mother see someone socially.
Maybe she and Adam could get the two back together again, a special
project. Her mother deserved some adult company.

"Bad news that I was so utterly selfish," she muttered. "Bad
that I didn't encourage Mama then with Mr. Bad Boy's dad. Bad on
me, but maybe I can fix that." The good news was that physically,
Diamond was feeling better and better. Pain and nausea seldom visited
her and, when they did, they soon left. She threw herself into studies.

One evening over dinner, Marsha passed her an envelope from
the local school district.

"Here, you open it, Mama."

"No, you."

Diamond stared at the envelope a bit before breaking the seal.
She read the letter, and her face lit up. She shrieked like a happy
banshee, shouting and strongly hugging her mother and grandmother.

Diamond couldn't believe it! Hunter College High School

was going to take her starting in January. She'd have all the rest of the summer and the coming fall to heal and to study with a tutor. She wasn't going to miss another grade. She'd begin as a second-semester freshman.

She wanted to call Adam, Tamara, and Shayna with the good news, but she hesitated. Tamara and Shayna . . . yeah, they'd be in the good school. But what about Adam? She'd never asked him how he did on the test. She'd never asked him if he was going to escape the bottom-of-the barrel school. God, she hoped Adora was stuck in the barrel.

She passed Diamond another envelope. It had three tickets to *Dream Girls* inside, a late October performance.

"Three?"

"From your cousins," Marsha answered. "One for me, one for you, and one for your Adam."

Life was getting much, much better.

The next night her mother brought a MacBook home, saying that her boss wanted Diamond to borrow it for awhile. The big booty super girl was overjoyed; but alone in her room with the laptop, she hesitated.

There were many ways the MacBook could improve her life, like email, iTunes, texts, downloading music, schoolwork, and learning more about bone marrow transplants. But all she really wanted was to log onto Facebook to read Adora's nasty posts. How could she resist?

She logged on, steeled herself and searched around, but found nothing insulting from Adora. So she changed her status post to: "Diamond's so, like, Hunter College High School, here I come!"

Then she settled down for some serious MacBook chat time with Adam, and was overjoyed to learn he'd also been accepted by Hunter. Having that computer connection reestablished their bond, and they emailed and texted day and night. By his next visit, they only had to wear the masks—and the following week they made a ritual out of removing their masks and kissing repeatedly. *Dream Girls* was only a month away.

Life was getting much, much, much better.

****

A few weeks later, Diamond was allowed to leave the apartment. It was way wonderful to go somewhere other than the hospital. She and Adam walked down to a Chinese restaurant, celebrating their acceptance into the good school by feeding each other bites of chicken and pork.

After dinner, there was a comic book movie, a huge popcorn feast, ample hand holding and, as a topper, a living feast of kissing (and petting) in the apartment. When Adam left, Diamond did her shake in front of the mirror. "Oh, yeah, the big booty Nuyorican super girl is home again—and locking lips with Mr. Bad Boy!"

Life was getting much, much, much, much better.

Diamond was too wound up to sleep. She lay awake reliving the night, the kisses, thinking of her future at high school with Adam. She marveled again at how good she felt, how whole and complete for the first time.

It has to be that bone marrow transplant. I mean, cause and effect. I'm actually getting better! Healthier!

Still, Diamond wanted to know who the donor was. Is it supermodel marrow? Some hockey player? Maybe somebody from the cast of *Smallville* or some soap opera.

I have a right to know, don't I? I have a right to find out the name of the soul that gave me a new lease on my life. I need to thank them.

She wanted to thank her kind donor in person, even if that meant a trip to Hollywood.

Abuela claimed not to know, but was not so convincing in her denials.

And her mother was clearly uncomfortable when asked about this. As Marsha fumbled out her denial, Diamond saw in her eyes a sadness she'd not seen before.

"You have an obligation to tell me, if you know. And you do know! I can tell that you know! How bad can it be? Maybe the donor wasn't famous in a good way. Was she a bank robber? A serial killer?

A porn star?" Oh, good lord, a porn star or a nude model for Playboy!

Her mother wouldn't tell her anything, but promised she'd contact the hospital and see what could be done. Barely speaking to each other, they left it at that.

Concerns about the donor vanished the very next day when Shayna and Tamara called to say that Adora was spreading a lie all over school that the only reason Diamond was accepted by Hunter College High School was because her mother was sleeping with the admissions director. "Everybody knows what a ho Marsha Lopez is," had apparently become Adora's mantra.

Adora, Tamara happily announced, was stuck in the bottom-of-the-barrel school.

Diamond was so devastated by Adora's posts that it overwhelmed her anger. What could she possibly do or say to let people know the truth? Nothing, she realized. She could only pray that her poor mother never found out bad things were being said about her, too. Diamond was baffled at why Adora would be so cruel, until she realized that it was probably because Adora was jealous! As painful as Adora's vicious attacks were, the thought of Adora being jealous of her made Diamond ecstatic.

What a strange mixture of happiness and misery!

She decided to make her own entry on Facebook: "What eighth grade skank is suing the city for building a sidewalk too close to her gigantic booty?"

Diamond's nickname for Adora became "Squatlow," and she learned that the dish at the softball field was how Squatlow, the cyber-bullying skank, was now getting cyber-bullied herself. Adora made a couple of pitiful responses and, little by little, she shrank into the background, her cyber bullying days over.

"I've trashed the skank at her own stupid game! Victory for the big booty Nuyorican super girl!" At the same time, Diamond felt a little ashamed that she'd stooped to Adora's level.

Diamond and Adam had the kind of Brooklyn end-of-August that was so fine it almost didn't seem real. They went to baseball games, kissed under the boardwalk, scarfed down hot dogs at Nathan's Famous and, a little further down Surf Avenue, they found an old-fashioned carousel where they got ten rides for two dollars. Diamond became a speed demon about catching the most rings.

The carousel's calliope sounds replaced the sounds of medical monitors, and became the theme music for Diamond and Adam.

****

During an early October trip to the hospital, Dr. Goldberg said the regular hospital visits could end and that Diamond only had to come back every six months. That afternoon, Diamond was doing her booty shake in front of the mirror in her Brooklyn bedroom.

All that marred Diamond's happiness were occasional spats with her mother about Adam seeming too serious too quickly, and about Marsha's refusal to talk about hospital bills and insurance and anything to do with finances.

The evening for *Dream Girls* came and went, but Diamond would remember it always.

On a cool November night, as she sat on her bed and read the new Storm comic, she heard her mother come into the apartment.

"Diamond, baby, would you please come in here?"

First time since the hospital she's called me baby; must be something important.

Diamond walked apprehensively into the living room and was surprised to see a strange man standing in the shadows by the front door. She took a couple more steps and saw tears in her mom's eyes.

"Mama, this is starting to weird me out. What's happening? Who..."

"Baby girl, this is someone I want you to meet."

Oh, please don't tell me this is your new "friend." Go back to Michael. He's much better looking.

The stranger took a few steps toward Diamond. She stared pointedly at his overly-thin face. Peering into his dark, deep-set eyes for only a moment, she found a truth.

She grabbed the arm of the couch, because she didn't trust her legs to hold her up. She could barely find her voice.

"Papa?"

"Hello, Diamond." His voice was softer than she'd imagined, not at all like the man at the Blind Pig bar from her dream in the hospital.

"You saved my life, Papa. Thank you . . ." She was at a loss for more words. She knew instantly that he was the donor. Not Beyoncé or a porn star or an opera singer or a famous outfielder for the Yankees. She didn't know what else to say to him.

He seemed to have the same problem because a long silence settled in the apartment. In it, the sounds of the city crept in . . . a car door slamming, someone shouting "get in here now for dinner," the clackity-clack of the subway, music from the apartment upstairs, some bluesy piece that sounded like Kenny G on the soprano sax.

"Come on, let's sit down," Marsha said. She gestured toward the kitchen and pulled out a chair for Larry. Diamond took in a deep breath, held it, and slowly exhaled. She couldn't stop staring at him.

"I can't believe it's really you . . . after all this time," Diamond said. "I wasn't sure you existed. I've spent my whole life thinking about you! I imagine that we're talking to each other all the time. I'd hear your voice in the music I played. You told me that you play guitar, and that you drive a Porsche. "

He gave her an odd smile.

"Is all that true? About the guitar and Porsche?"

She didn't give him a chance to answer. "Why didn't you ever come to see me? Where have you lived all this time? Why . . ." Her questions came rapid fire now, and it seemed like there would never be enough time in the world for all of them to be answered.

"We have a lot to catch up on," Larry interrupted. "Diamond, I'm sorry I was never there for you. I was young and stupid when you were born, and I had a lot of problems that I didn't deal with very well. I'm not proud of the life I've lived. But it was a miracle that your mother found me and gave me a chance to help you. It made me proud of both of us and, in a way, it saved *my* life too. That's it, Diamond, I didn't save you . . . you saved me."

Diamond considered his words for a moment, as her eyes filled with tears.

"It's a start, isn't it, Papa? I guess we really *are* helping each other. Everybody deserves second chances, and you gave me the biggest second chance a person could ever have. I'm so grateful for that."

"Then maybe you and your mother can give me a second chance, too."

They continued their conversation late into the night, sharing a fresh *tres leches* cake that Abuela had baked.

"I'd like to come back if you'll have me," Larry said.

Marsha smiled weakly and looked at their daughter

uncomfortably. "We'll have to talk about this later."

Larry turned to Diamond. "I don't drive a Porsche," he said. "I don't even own a car. Is that okay?"

Diamond just hugged him and replied, "I'm so glad to finally meet you. . . " Marsha interjected, "Larry, thank you for coming through this time. We all have a lot to talk about. But, let's do it at another time," and escorted him to the door. They embraced each other briefly and he was gone.

Diamond wandered to her room in a daze of dreams with too much on her mind to fall asleep that night. She had waited all her life, yearning for this moment that perhaps she thought might never happen. Diamond used to imagine being reunited with her Dad to be like a scene from one of the telenovela soap operas that her Abuela watched on Telemundo.

"We would pick up where we never left off. There'd be daddy/ daughter dances and all the corny stuff dads and daughters are supposed to do. He'd be intensely interested in me and protective too, just showering me with love, attention and expensive gifts. The minute Papa saw me, he'd start to cry from being so happy and hug me so tightly as if he'd never let me go. And like the end of each telenovela, everything would be resolved with warm embraces, tears of joy and toasting to our new life as a family with mojitos and sangria."

Instead, Diamond had a mixed bag of confusion—she found

her papa and he saved her life as only he could do. But he wasn't even close to what she had imagined. Then, she gazed out her window, trying to find an answer through her limited view of the beach.

"New York is like a diamond of many facets. Everything sparkles from the lights of Broadway, Times Square, Radio City Music Hall, Rockefeller Center to the Wonder Wheel's neon lights and the people who bring the city to life every moment of every day. We make this city shine. We are the true stars. New York has been called the City that never sleeps—maybe it's 'cause everyone is working so hard to sparkle."

Diamond then realized her namesake for what it really meant— sparkling no matter what life has to offer and sharing your radiance with others.

MICHELE AMIRA was 11 years old when she learned to read and write. She was only 14 years old when she was contracted to write *Sparkle*—the same age as Diamond in the story. *Sparkle* is based on the young author's own struggles and victories, fighting a rare life-threatening illness, confronting bullying, dealing with school and just being a teen. Profits from *Sparkle* will be contributed to Beauty & Quality of Life, a program she created and oversees to help other teens like herself (and Diamond) who battle life-threatening illnesses. Today, Michele is a professional hip-hop journalist, radio DJ, stand-up comedian and student. She is also vegan dancer with a love of hair products, hoop earrings, hip-hop, and New York pizza! When she's not writing about what's hot in hip-hop, she's talking about it on her hip-hop radio show, *The Mecca*, at University of Maryland where she is an English major. She has been published in *The New York Times*, *The Source Magazine*, MTV's *Pardon My Blog*, *JVibe Magazine*, Fran Drescher's Cancerschmancer's "*We The Future*" blog and other notable publications. She is the youngest filmmaker to be screened at The Festival de Cannes in France. She is also the recipient of the Spirit of Anne Frank Student Award and featured in *Bethesda Magazine* as one of the Nation's Top Teens. Most of all, she loves to inspire others to "sparkle."

The Music in Me Foundation Int'l

About Us

Our mission is to reduce the literacy gap among disadvantaged youth, prevent bullying, build self-esteem and eliminate self-limitation by providing fun multimedia arts presentations, teaching language arts through arts integration, inspiring children's literature, and providing an engaging digital platform designed to provide teachers, counselors, administrators and parents with a meaningful measurement tool and data collection system to help students discover "their music" or strengths. Our innovative program is truly a first of its kind, which is a holistic approach to education that reaches all students through the arts. Its multi-modality method uses all forms of learning styles and communication approaches so that students can learn in the way they're wired. We're currently working with thousands of school-aged children per week. Our goal is to expand globally to reach as many children as possible. We have a three-pronged approach to our program:

1. "Rap" on Reading Book Series
2. "Unleash Your Superpowers" Multimedia Show and Programs
3. The Music in Me Interactive Digital Platform

Using the same "Music in Me" philosophy that led my children to achieve enormous success in spite of struggling with challenges, we are determined to spread The Music in Me's special brand of hope and inspiration to youth by helping them discover their unique "superpowers" to obtain their dreams and free themselves from self-limitation.

smiles –
Jane Pinczuk

Founder & CEO, The Music in Me Foundation Int'l
(949) 371-9055 www.themusicinme.org

Beauty of Life & Quality of Life

Ambassador Big Sean

Beauty of Life & Quality of Life currently provides teen girls in the Washington Metropolitan Area fighting life-threatening illnesses like cancer, gastrointestinal diseases, blood disorders and cystic fibrosis, as well as other chronic and terminal diseases, with hope and a chance to "sparkle." The concept of this program was born through my personal experiences fighting a rare life-threatening autoimmune gastrointestinal disease. When my peers were going to prom and sleepovers, I was getting blood transfusions.

Beauty of Life & Quality of Life enables young girls and teens battling illnesses to feel beautiful inside and out while enduring harsh side effects like hair loss and weight changes – even during long hospital stays. We accomplish our mission through special events and girly swag bags full of feel-good items like cosmetics, jewelry, iTunes Gift Cards, autographed copies of *Sparkle*, cuddly items and so much more. We donate hundreds of girly swag bags to the hematology, oncology, surgery and gastrointestinal units of Children's National Medical Center, The Transplant Center for Children at Georgetown University Hospital and Simcha Chai Lifeline Camps. It is my goal to extend our reach into other Children's Miracle Network Hospitals and camps in other areas across the country.

15336507R00154

Made in the USA
San Bernardino, CA
23 September 2014